Beauty

Rising

A Novel

By

Mark W. Sasse

For my family,
who made all those years in Vietnam unforgettable.

ACKNOWLEDGMENTS

Special thanks to my wife, Karen, and my other readers Sandy, Jo, and Abbie who all gave me valuable insight and suggestions.

Part I

My Life as Martin Kinney Jr.

The Wallet

The crowd pressed in from every side making me extremely self-conscious of my wallet, which was still in the back right pocket of my jeans. I stood in a sea of black haired people being the only red-head, and my Steelers cap did little to mask that fact. The smell of incense lingered everywhere and the non-syncopated drum beat seemed to push the smoke from the man-sized joss sticks in random directions. Everything looked random. Everything felt random. I could barely see my taxi driver, who was separated from me by nearly ten people, half of whom cut through the scene towards me and the other half who weaved beside and in front of me. Through the chaos there was continual movement but little progress. I continued stepping on toes and plowed through the congestion trying to catch up with my thin, short Vietnamese driver. I placed my hand firmly over my wallet in my back jeans pocket and waited for an opening slightly larger than my big frame that would enable me to remove my wallet so that I could slide it into my front pocket. Suddenly, a violent push from behind jerked me forward nearly knocking over the gaunt old woman wearing a conical hat in front of me. I immediately returned my hand over my back pocket, but it was empty. The wallet was gone. I frantically turned around looking at the crowd which cornered me from every angle, and I reached out and grabbed the arm of a young Vietnamese woman immediately on my right.

"Where's my wallet? Give me my wallet," I yelled at her.

She looked in horror at me; I had either frightened her to death, or the con was on. Her face looked so young, so smooth; so frail. I felt like a big white bully picking on a helpless girl. Maybe it was her beautiful guile that sucked me in as Vietnam always does with America. She was beautiful, with long black flowing hair just like dad said. People continued to whip around us in all directions as she stood staring at me pulling and straining as I firmly held her wrist. She was a slender deer meant for sprinting; I was the hunter who trapped her. I didn't know if she was the thief. There was no way to tell. If she could only give me a smile, like the girl that smiled at my dad under the banana tree, then I might know something. I felt like I held her wrist forever, and she only stared back in terror, looking deep into me with those black innocent looking eyes. I had to let go, so I released her. Her white flowing clothes disappeared through the crowd like a vapor. I stood completely alone, moneyless, in the midst of a thousand people in this strange, exotic land. At least I had done what dad had asked. That was the only comfort I had.

A Father to Me

"Martin, close the door."

I did. My dad was taciturn to the extreme. We never communicated about anything, except when he felt the need to bully his whims on my soul, which had been nearly every day of my life. I dreaded closed door conversations. They never turned out well.

"Come closer. Sit here."

I pulled the wooden desk chair from the corner and sat flopping about uncomfortably shifting from one side to the other. My dad's voice seemed stronger than usual, but he looked pale. He removed the oxygen tubes out of his nose and painfully tried to lift himself so he could sit up. I leaned forward to lend a hand.

"Just sit," he barked angrily not letting me touch him.

I sat back down and the wooden chair rocked once to the left thudding on the wood floor.

"Martin. I—"

My mom opened the door suddenly.

"What are you doing in there Martin? Get out of here. Your father needs his rest."

"Woman, leave us alone. Martin, sit back down."

I sat twisted between a hurricane and a tornado.

"Leave us!" my father yelled at my mother. She glared at me and slammed the door as she left. The silence reverberated for a second. The tension felt normal. Dad cleared his throat and leaned back on his pillow.

"Martin, I'm dying. Soon."

We all knew it. I didn't know what to feel. I wouldn't miss his drunkenness, or his insults; I wouldn't miss how he picked on every little thing my mother did; I wouldn't miss how my mom would slap him silly when he came home drunk making him sleep it off on the living room floor. He was my father, but I wasn't sure if there was anything I would miss about him.

"Martin, I haven't been a very good father."

I strained to recognize the words. They seemed foreign.

"Just don't say anything. I should have been more of a father to you. I shouldn't have been so hard on you."

He placed his head back against his pillow and swore. I always hated his vulgar mouth.

"Martin, will you do something for me? I don't feel like I have a right to ask you this, but will you do something for me?"

"Of course, Dad. Whatever you want," I eagerly edged forward. My eyes felt like they were swelling, but I twitched my hands back and forth determined not to rub them.

"Nam. I was nineteen in April 1969. I was in Tay Nguyen – central highlands. We hadn't seen any action for a couple days. We were stationed outside Ban Me Thuot. I was out there with two of my buddies Johnson and

Newbert. We were just pissing around trying to kill some time. There was this beautiful lake, kind of reminded me of Lake Arthur, except for the vast expanse of banana trees on the one side and peasants with their conical hats on the other. So Johnson and Newbert decide to take a swim. They stripped down to nothing and jump in like a bunch of school boys. I told them I'd be right behind them after I go cut a bunch of bananas out of a tree. I walked down about hundred yards weaving through the trees, and these large leaves kept smacking me in the face. I found this nice bunch of bananas just slightly ripe, and I pulled out my army knife and started slashing through the limb when sitting on this large rock which jutted out of the bank just ten feet from where I stood was this girl – the most beautiful girl I ever saw in my life. Long black hair down to her waist. She just sat there staring at me."

My dad stopped the story, coughed twice, and took a sip of water from the bedside stand. I didn't know what to make of his story. I had never heard him talk once about Vietnam except for all the BS drinking and war stories he would whoop up when his Vet brothers came around.

"She smiled at me and then motioned for me to come sit by her. I swear to God she motioned for me to come to her," he said in a lazy, dreamy voice. "This was one of those 'too good to be true' moments – the kind that happen so infrequently during war that you just believe you're dreaming. And so it was, I was dreaming, and she was waving at me to come and sit by her. I don't know what she said to me in Vietnamese, but I just sat right down and talked right back."

He stared off into the blank white wall for a while, and I could tell he felt a bit of relief. His mind glimpsed something far beyond the reach of lowly little Lyndora.

"She ah, well she kissed me, and then shied back a few feet. Well, I would have been a fool not to know what she wanted. Why she wanted it, I never knew to this day. But you didn't question gifts back then – not in that hell hole. And so we did it, right there in the banana grove just out of earshot of my buddies."

I had no idea why he was telling me this. I also had no idea if what he said was true. He always lied about everything, but it was the most he ever said to me in years. He spoke with an unfamiliar emotion almost bordering on happiness. I didn't know what to say or how to react, so I sat quietly, eagerly waiting to see where this story was going. I could not imagine my dad as a nineteen year old; nor could I imagine him with a beautiful young woman.

"So you know, after a while we said our pleasantries, and I reached out to touch her face one last time. I had to make sure she was real. Her skin was so soft without any blemish. And I kissed her one last time. Then she stood up and ran up over the hill. She was in white – all white. And she disappeared like a ghost or maybe like an angel. I felt drunk and stumbled back down toward the lake. The guys were getting dressed and started asking me where I had been. When I told them, they got all over my case accusing me of lying to them. I pleaded with them that I told them the truth, but they continued to shake their heads and push me around trying to see or not if I had really been the luckiest guy in the world. They continued ranting and raging as we grabbed our gear and started trekking over towards the rice fields to meet up with the rest of our unit about a mile or so up the road."

He stopped. His face turned grim and his eyes intense.

"A second later, a bullet rips right through Newbert's head. It just exploded, and blood shot everywhere. We hit the ground right before Newbert's lifeless body plopped between us. His eyes stared at me. Johnson yelled at me that we had to get out of there, that there wasn't any cover from the sniper. He said we had to get over the ridge of the rice field. But I just laid there looking at Newbert staring at me. His eyes seemed to bulge out. He had a huge hole right behind his left ear. We didn't know where the sniper was, but Johnson was right. We were sitting ducks. Johnson yelled non-stop at me, but I couldn't make sense of what he was saying until I suddenly heard the word 'now'. He got up and started running, and I was not two steps behind him. Another shot rang out as we headed toward the first rice paddy. If we could get over the first embankment we'd at least have some protection."

He stopped again. I had for a moment forgotten where I was. It wasn't my father I was listening to. Not the father I knew. It was someone magical, unbelievable. Someone I wanted to hear more from. Someone I didn't want to die.

"And then," his voice broke up and tears began streaming down his face – the face of a stranger. "Johnson jumped up over the embankment and into the rice field and," he paused again. "He disappeared. The rice field swallowed him. He sank. The hell-hole of Vietnam swallowed him up."

I didn't know what he was talking about. But he paused for a long time and wiped his face, coughing a few times. He was severely agitated. His right hand shook up and down.

"Do you have a cigarette?"

"Dad, the doctor said…"

"I don't care what the doctor said, I'm dying. Ah…" He leaned back again and took a deep breath. "You see, he had jumped right into a B52 shell hole. He was killed by his own army. Those B52s would rip a huge hole out of the ground. When it happened to be in a rice paddy, the flooded field would cover right over the damn hole. It was completely invisible. Then along comes some sorry sack like Johnson, and he hops right into the hole with a seventy pound pack on his back and sinks right to the bottom, drowning in five seconds. I had jumped over too but hung onto the side of the embankment after I saw Johnson go under. I shimmied over about twenty yards and carefully slid down feeling with my legs to see if there was dirt under the paddy water or not. There was, and so I curled myself up in a ball and just laid there in the mud and water for hours. I thought about Newbert, and I vomited all over myself. Then I thought about Johnson laying just fifty feet away at the bottom of the shell hole. Get it. Shell hole. Hell hole. All the same. I wished I was in the hole with him. Then I thought of that girl – the angel. Her skin. Dark and soft. So smooth. It had to have been a dream. I longed for her to come to the paddy. I longed for her to be with me in the mud and water. I longed to stay with her forever. She was so beautiful. I have never forgotten her face."

He looked so white, like he was living his last breath. I felt as if he was talking the life right out of him.

"After dark, I finally got up out of the mud, climbed up

the embankment and weaved my way through the fields toward the flickering lights to the north. I don't really remember walking back to my unit, but I remember getting there and telling my commander about Newbert and Johnson. He told me we'd need to go out in the morning to find their bodies. You know, before that night I never drank a lick of alcohol in my life. Your grandma went to the Methodist church over on Main. She would have whipped me if I ever tried the stuff here in Lyndora."

Two images I couldn't grasp – my dad going to church and my dad not drinking.

"But that night I had a whole lot of whiskey. A whole lot," he faded out for a moment. "A whole lot. Martin, that was the last day of my life. There in the banana trees, that was the last time I ever lived. I've been dragging you and your mother through the muddy rice paddies of Vietnam for 40 years. I married, I had a child, and I've lived my whole life in this town, but I left everything in that hell-hole of Vietnam. My future wife, my future child, my religion – they all drowned with Johnson that day. They all sank with him and laid there on the bottom."

Dad paused again, but he had barely any expression on his face at all.

"Martin, I've been a terrible father."

"No, Dad," I tried to say something encouraging to him, but he glared at me with venomous eyes as if he would not accept any more lies in this house. Not on his death bed. He would not be comforted; especially not from the one he hurt the most. I couldn't hold the tears back anymore, and I wiped my eyes ferociously trying to hide them.

"Martin, will you do one thing for me?"

"Anything Dad. Anything."

"I want to be cremated. I want you to take my ashes to Tay Nguyen. Find the little lake just southeast of Ban Me Thuot and pour my ashes between the banana trees. Will you do that for me son?"

"I will."

"Your mother won't allow it. She will try and…"

I stopped him before he could say another word. I knew what he would say, and I knew he was right. My mother would never allow me to go. Even though I have celebrated thirty six birthdays, I had hardly grown into a man. I knew it. There was never any time to grow up in this house. I was a thirty-six-year-old junk food eating child, who let his mother belittle him and his father make fun of him. I had never even been across the Pennsylvania border let alone in a foreign country. I worked in the stockroom of K-Mart for the last nine years. I spent Tuesday nights bowling and Sunday afternoons watching NASCAR.   I hadn't had a real talk with a girl in ten years. Hadn't dated one in fifteen. I was 250 pounds with a scraggly red beard. I was convinced that besides Tuesdays and Sundays I had the most miserable existence in the world. I was the buffer between two people who hated each other for as long as I could remember. Now this stranger – this father I never knew – was leaving me by telling me stories that made it all somehow make sense. He had died in Vietnam. I was another consequence of the war – a by-product of a time period that nearly drowned a whole generation.

"Dad, don't worry. I'll do it. You can count on me."

Then he looked at me and said something else so strange, so wonderful, so life giving that I couldn't help but cry some more.

"Thank you, son."

The Lake

The taxi driving kept saying "Nui Coc, Nui Coc".

"I need to find the lake of 'Thai Win'," I kept saying repeatedly.

"Nui Coc, Nui Coc. Lake of Thai Nguyen. Here it is. Only lake in Thai Nguyen."

My emotions struck me hard. The sight of the water pierced my stomach. I don't know if my father really believed me – that I would actually come to Vietnam and fulfill his wish. I got out of the car and looked at the rolling hills around the lake, thick with trees. It was truly beautiful and so serene. I imagined my father as a young man trudging through the countryside, finding the girl that smiled at him; the girl that randomly invited him to leave his soul here. I imagined him kissing the girl goodbye and telling his naked swimming friends about his encounter. I imagined them telling him to stop his BS and excitedly trying to make him come clean with the truth. Then I imagined Newbert taking the bullet in the head. It was so peaceful now. Everything seemed unreal.

"Where are the rice fields?" I asked the driver. This

was not the spot; it was too hilly, and there were no
banana trees.

"What?" asked the driver.

"Are there some rice fields around here? I need to
find some rice fields on the edge of the lake."

The driver looked completely perplexed.

"You want to go down to city; we see rice fields. I
know good restaurant too. You hungry? Eat?" he
replicated the eating motion with his hands and mouth.

"No. I need rice fields. Or banana trees. Rice fields or
banana trees by the lake."

We drove around for another thirty minutes; forested
hills spread out in all directions. As we approached what
must have been the northern tip of the lake, we pulled off
to the side and the driver led me down through a small
grove that covered the embankment heading down to the
lake. When we reached the water, I looked out and saw a
low expanse of land leading off into the horizon, and on
the far side stood a large grove of banana trees. My heart
pounded, *could this be it?* There were not any rice fields,
but perhaps this land used to have them? It was over forty
years ago. I trudged along the edge of the lake. The
ground was soft and my shoes quickly began sinking into
the mud, but I kept moving. *Could this really be the spot?*
Would there be a large rock jutting out like my dad said? I
reached the edge of the banana grove. There was no one
around. The driver squatted by the edge of the lake,
smoking, about a quarter of a mile away. The trees were
full of green banana bunches. I started walking up through
the grove looking intently for any rock that could fit the
description. The ground was smooth, but damp. My
shoes were completely black with mud. I scoured the

entire grove over and over. There was no rock. There were no rice fields. But could this still have been the place. After all, it was the only lake in Thai Win and these were the only banana trees we could find around the lake. I went down to the beginning of the grove and sat flat right in the moist dirt. Removing my backpack, I pulled out the Rubbermaid container that held the ashes.

"Dad. I did the best I could."

I looked down at the remains.

"I know you never thought I would amount to anything. You were always disappointed in me. But look Dad, I'm in Vietnam. I've never even crossed into Ohio, and now I'm sitting under a banana tree in Vietnam. Dad, I did it."

I couldn't hold it in any longer. The tears flowed, like every other night when I was young in my bedroom listening to dad yell at mom.

"It doesn't matter Dad. It doesn't matter. I'm here. I'm here for you."

I unsealed the red lid on the two quart container when suddenly a light wind blew ashes all over my jeans.

"Ahh," I jumped up wiping my pants with my left hand while balancing the Rubbermaid top over the container in my right.

"I can't even dump out ashes. Idiot."

I backed up two feet when a banana tree branch pierced through my right hand and knocked the Rubbermaid onto the ground, dumping the ashes all over. I stood frozen, having a hard time believing what I just did, though I wasn't totally surprised.

"Sorry, Dad. You know I've always been a little clumsy. Sorry. But I made it, Dad. I made it to Vietnam."

Cremation

Dad died the morning after he told me his Vietnam story. Mom didn't react or say much of anything. I went for a walk. I stopped in front of the Methodist church on Main Street and thought about young dad and grandma walking through the arched front doors on a Sunday morning. The parsonage was set off to the side about a hundred feet further back from the street than the church. I walked right up the three cinderblocks used as steps for the front door and knocked firmly. I felt especially calm. An elderly man with a bald head and a rim of white hair from ear to ear smiled as he opened the wooden door.

"Hello, son. What can I do for you?"

"Hello, Reverend. My name is Martin Kinney Jr. My family lives over on Home Avenue."

"You're a Kinney. Martin Kinney, you say. Well I know your father. Or knew your father a long, long time ago. Come in, come in. I'm so glad you came. Your father is still a member here – inactive that is. But we never close the doors on reconciliation."

He brought me into his small living room. There was

a red painted piano in the corner and a well-worn sofa opposite it where he sat me down as I pondered the shocking fact of my father being a church member.

"So how is your father Martin?"

"He died this morning," I said without any emotion. I still didn't know what I felt.

"Oh Martin, I am sorry. How could I be of assistance to your family during this time?"

"I never knew my Dad had ever gone to church. But last night, he was talking to me about when he was a boy and he said my grandma would take him every Sunday."

"Maggie. You must have never met your grandmother, is that right, Martin?"

"Yes sir, that's right. She died when I was one year old."

"I came here in 1960. Your father must have been about ten years old at the time. Your grandmother was a Godly woman. Never missed a service. She sang in the choir and directed the Christmas pageant for years; in fact, I believe it was my first Christmas here when your father sang a solo in the pageant."

"My father, sing?"

"Well, that was a long time ago."

"Reverend, would you come and say a few words at my father's funeral?"

"Martin, of course I will," he paused thoughtfully looking straight into my eyes. "Would you like me to take care of the whole funeral service?"

I nodded gratefully.

"Fine. I'll take care of it. Just give me the details."

———————————

By the time I arrived home, the funeral assistant was at the house talking to Mom in the kitchen.

"Mr. Baldwin, I'll be in this afternoon to pick out the casket," I heard my Mom say to the short man all dressed in black.

"Very well, Mrs. Kinney."

Neither acknowledged me as I stood in the doorway.

"No," I spoke boldly. "No casket. Dad's being cremated."

My Mom twirled her head around and looked at me. Her eyebrows seemed to be permanently in the downward position for years now. I was used to this scowl, but I would not be moved.

"Martin, take the trash out. We are busy here," she turned back to Mr. Baldwin. "Is 3:30 okay?"

"Yes, that would be fine, Mrs. Kinney."

"No, Mom. You don't understand. Dad must be cremated."

"Martin, shut up!" She blushed mildly then turned back to Mr. Baldwin feigning a grin to cover over her harsh tone. "He just doesn't know what he's talking about."

I ignored her and walked up to Mr. Baldwin. He uncomfortably smiled my way as I approached. The cremation would happen. I would see to it.

"Mr. Baldwin, it was my father's wish to be cremated…"

"Martin. He said no such thing. Mr. Baldwin, I'm sorry for this distraction. He's always butting his nose into things," she said sourly.

"Mr. Baldwin, he wanted to be cremated, so could you please arrange that? Also, could you notify Reverend Fox at the Methodist church over on Main Street about the funeral arrangements? I've asked him to say a few words and organize it for us."

"Reverend Fox? What the hell are you talking about? I will not have that man step foot in the funeral service. Just what are you trying to do? Martin, leave!"

"Mom."

"Martin, I have had enough of you. Can you not respect my wishes just this once? Even on the day of my husband's death?" Her voice rose sharply. "Get out of here and stop this nonsense."

Mr. Baldwin cowered by the refrigerator. Our kitchen was so small that a twosome fighting took up nearly the whole room.

"So, what would you like me to do?" Mr. Baldwin interjected.

"Cremation," I said deliberately at him.

This lit the fuse, and the explosion sure enough followed. Mom got into my face yelling every type of obscenity – the kind I had heard all before. Too many times. They didn't pierce as deep or cut so easily. I walked to the counter for a glass as my mother hung onto me with her verbal assault. I ignored her. What she said didn't matter. What she felt didn't matter. What Mr. Baldwin thought of our relationship certainly didn't matter. I walked back to the refrigerator and poured myself a glass of milk. Mr. Baldwin hovered over me from my left; my mother's assault continued from the right. As I lifted my glass to my mouth, my mother grabbed it out of my hand and hurled it across the room. The glass sailed over the table and smashed through the kitchen window which overlooked the back porch. Glass splintered onto the table, though most of it was caught up in the thin cotton curtains. Everything stopped for a moment. My mother quieted down and backed up a step away from my ear. Mr. Baldwin rubbed his hands against his pants, fidgeting terribly. I looked at my mother. Her scowl stared at me but did not penetrate. I was remarkably calm.

"Mom, if you would just listen to me. Dad told me last night what his wishes were. And I will honor them. I am no longer your little boy. I'm a man, Mom. I'm a man. Don't you know how old I am?"

A show of truth and emotion rarely heard by these four walls.

"So you can rant and rave. You can swear at me and call me stupid. But for the first time ever, my Dad gave me a simple request – a heartfelt request. You can hate me for the rest of my life, but Dad is being cremated."

Mom started crying. She turned around without a word and headed for the staircase.

"And Reverend Fox is speaking at the funeral," I yelled after her then turned back to Mr. Baldwin who stood flatfooted but surely eager to charge out the door. "Mr. Baldwin, I'm sorry about all of this. It's been kind of crazy around here lately. Can you make the necessary arrangements for the cremation?"

"Sure. Yes. I'll take care of it."

"And you can talk with Reverend Fox about the memorial service?"

"I will," Mr. Baldwin said. "Do you want the service at the funeral home?"

"No. Why don't we have it at the church?"

At the Police Station

The taxi driver rescued me from the throngs of people who continually wore me down with their concentrated stares. A visibly irritated 250 pound red-headed white man garnered an obscene amount of attention. Between the little boys who would come and pull the hairs on my arms and the girls who overloaded me with 'What your name?', 'hello, hello', 'where you fum' I experienced in a matter of minutes a lifetime's worth of attention that I would have received on Home Avenue in Lyndora. The girl whom I held in my grasp was long gone as was my wallet. I felt so alone, except for the annoying taxi driver. He was happy I had already prepaid him, and I actually felt happy that he was still with me.

"Just down here is police station. You can tell them."

We walked through the crowd; eyes were stuck all over me. Several people grabbed my gut. Little girls giggled at me and pointed at my hair. Hawkers selling everything from joss sticks to banana leaf wrapped rice hung all over me. I was a broke foreigner. A hawker's worst nightmare. The taxi driver kept pulling me along.

"Where was your wallet?"

"In my back pocket."

"That's stupid. Don't put it in your back pocket."

"I know."

"If you know, why you do?"

Shut up I thought.

At the end of the dirt street sat a two story, mustard colored cement building which was the local police office. Tan, my driver, took me in the front door. There were several desks sprawled out on both sides of the room with about ten policemen in their drab green uniforms huddled around a couple different computers. They were drinking tea and watching a local drama on TV. Two of them stood up and barked out what sounded like some commands to Tan. Tan talked furiously at them pointing back to me from time to time. The two officers laughed, and then smiled at me which perked up the attention of the rest of the officers.

"They want to know where you are from."

"America."

"America. Number 1," one of the policemen said with a grin. He then exchanged words with Tan.

"They want to know what you are doing in Thai Nguyen."

"My father was a soldier during the Vietnam War. He recently died, and I wanted to come see where he served."

Tan translated it back to the officers who now looked a little perplexed.

"Your father. He a pilot? Airplane?" Tan asked.

"No. He was a soldier. Infantry."

The Vietnamese exchanged more information.

"Your father, was he American?"

I looked at Tan strangely.

"Of course he was American. Are they going to help me with my wallet?" I began to think that everyone around was nothing but a useless idiot. What silly questions to ask? Do I seriously look like I could have had a Vietnamese father with this height, weight, and pasty-white skin?

"They said you are in the wrong place."

"No, I'm not. There was a theft. They are police."

"No, no. Not about wallet. You father not in Thai Nguyen."

"My Dad specifically said he was in Thai Win."

They chatted some more in Vietnamese when one of the officers quickly got excited. His voice raised and he laughed furiously while the others joined in.

"What's so funny?" I asked.

"Why no you tell me your father was a soldier? Then you don't get your wallet stolen."

"What are you talking about?"

"Your father no say 'Thai Nguyen' he said 'Tay Nguyen'."

"Huh?"

"This is Thai Nguyen. No American soldiers ever in Thai Nguyen. Tay Nguyen is in the south. Lots of American soldiers in the south during war. No soldiers here. Your father never here."

I didn't know what to say. I looked around grasping at something to say. Could it really be true? Did I make a colossal mistake?

"Here, look," Tan pointed over to a map of Vietnam that was pinned onto a cork board. "Here, the capital Hanoi. You fly into the capital today. We travel north to

Thai Nguyen – you say you want to find lake in Thai Nguyen. See here. Lake Nui Coc. Then I take you to cultural festival here. Chua Hang. This is north. But look, Tay Nguyen way down here. Highlands in the south. Lots of American soldiers there during the war. No soldiers in the north. You in the wrong place. You go to the right place, nobody steals your wallet today. Bad luck day."

My heart sank. I dumped my father's ashes in the heart of communist Vietnam – over a thousand miles from the death of his comrades – over a thousand miles from the smile of that girl. How could I have been so stupid? Didn't my dad know that I got D's in history? Of course he didn't. He never looked at my report cards. All he gave me was a simple request, but only I could mess it up this big. I deserved every one of my parents' insults. I was an idiot. I was the biggest idiot ever. Everyone in the police station was having a good time – except me. Why did I even come here? Why didn't we just bury him like normal people? Why did I have to step in? Why didn't I let Mom take care of everything as she always did? I finally found enough of a voice to speak up.

"How about my wallet?"

Tan turned back to the officers and talked for a moment. Their excited expressions kept their intensity as they kept smiling and laughing.

"Wallet gone. You will never find it. You can fill out police report if you want, but it waste time. You never get wallet again. Do you have any other money?"

"No."

"Credit card?"

"No."

"You in trouble."

The Funeral

Mom gave in. She stepped back from all the arrangements and made me do everything. I didn't mind at all. In fact, it was some of the best quality time I ever had with my father. The last time I felt this close to him was when we went to Conneaut Lake when I was seven. I still have the photo of us each holding cotton candy, and he had his arm around me, smiling. Was that really the last good memory of my father? I didn't want to think about it. I just wanted to get through the funeral.

Mr. Baldwin made the arrangements for Saturday morning, three days after dad's death. Mom barely spoke a word to me during those three days. I spent Friday morning at the mall trying to find a black suit that would fit me. My everyday wardrobe consisted of forty-seven t-shirts and four pairs of jeans which I wore in a cyclical manner. I was comfortable in every piece of clothing that makes itself at home in a bowling alley. But for dad's funeral, I wanted to do it right, so I bought a two piece suit, trimmed my beard, and got a haircut.

At about 9:30 on Saturday morning, Mom, in her black

dress, and I, in my black suit, walked out of the house and started our silent march to the church which was just two blocks away.

"Mom."

She didn't respond.

"Are you still mad at me?"

What frivolous questions I had in my mind.

We continued our walk until we arrived at the Methodist church. The front door was unlocked, so we walked in to see Reverend Fox milling about in the front.

"Mrs. Kinney. Martin. Please come up front so we can talk about the service. Mrs. Kinney, please accept my sincere condolences on the passing of your husband."

Mom glanced once right into Reverend Fox's face and then continued right past him and sat in the front pew of the aisle on the left. She did nothing to acknowledge Reverend Fox. I couldn't believe how incredibly rude and insensitive she was – even if it was her husband's funeral.

"I'm sorry, Reverend. My Mom hasn't been herself lately," I whispered knowing full well I just told a white lie in church. She was, in fact, feeling every bit herself.

"Martin, it's okay. Everyone grieves in their own way. I've learned not to take things so personally because a funeral is a very trying time indeed. You just be there for your mother. She'll need you."

I nodded, acknowledging what he said but could not believe it. I kept my eyes on my Mom as Reverend Fox went over the particulars of the funeral. She unflinchingly kept her eyes forward perhaps staring at the urn, which had been placed on the communion table below the raised pulpit. I couldn't wait for everything to be over. I couldn't wait to make my arrangements for Vietnam even though I knew another battle with mom loomed on the horizon. She would never understand, and I could never tell her the truth about why I had to go to Vietnam. It would break her heart to know that dad had a good memory that she didn't share. Perhaps his only good memory. She must have still loved him at some level in some way.

By ten till ten, around thirty people had entered the church for the memorial service. Our neighbors the Dombroskis and Allens greeted me and my mom in the front row and then settled into some pews about halfway back. There were a few people from dad's work and a couple of his Vet brothers. My Aunt Alice and her two older sons came and sat behind us. My dad was a gruff and vulgar man, though not completely unlikeable outside his own home.

Precisely at ten o'clock, Reverend Fox ascended to the podium to conduct the memorial service. It no doubt would be short. I had informed him that neither I nor my Mom wanted to say anything, so it was completely up to him. Perhaps it was bizarre to have a stranger give a eulogy, but it would have been insincere to have one of us try to sugarcoat my dad's life. It was what it was; and that being true, it was better left unsaid.

"Ladies and gentlemen, we are gathered here today to pay our last respects to Martin J. Kinney."

Our only respects I thought.

"I first would like to offer my sincere condolences to Martin's surviving family members Mrs. Jane Kinney and Martin Jr. When Martin Jr. asked me to say a few words, I couldn't help but think of the young Martin Kinney I knew many, many years ago. I came to this church as an assistant pastor in 1960. I was just out of seminary only twenty-one years old. Martin was ten years old at the time and faithfully came to church each week with his mother Maggie – Maggie Kinney. Maggie was a rip-roaring soul for Jesus. Her cup runneth over with enthusiasm for church if you know what I mean. She organized the Christmas pageant year after year. She taught children's Sunday School for nearly twenty years, and she volunteered regularly in the community. The young Martin certainly followed after his mother's fervor."

The Reverend was laying it on too thick for my taste. Mom sat expressionless. I could only imagine what she thought of this line of story-telling. It seemed to be the most obtuse piece of fiction in the universe – out of the mouth of a saint. How unseemly. Yet I appreciated Reverend Fox's attempt to keep the funeral civil and respectful.

"I remember my first Christmas here; Martin sang a solo at the Christmas pageant – *The Little Drummer Boy*. Actually, I was going through some of the church's old photos, and I came across this photo of Martin singing. I'd like to give this to Martin Jr."

Reverend Fox stepped down from the pulpit and handed me the photo. A young Martin Kinney wore a white shirt with a bright red vest over top of it. He stood at a microphone with wide eyes and an open mouth. His light red hair was parted on the side. Mom didn't even glance my way. I gazed at the boy – the innocent boy of another lifetime – the boy who had yet to experience Vietnam or the girl under the banana tree or the hole through Newbert's head. He sang *Little Drummer Boy*; he must have just finished 'rum-pa-pum-pum' as someone snapped the picture. The picture engrossed me, swallowed me, overcame me. It drowned me like the B52 hole in Vietnam drowned Johnson. I felt trapped by this picture. It was much too unfair to look at it, to ponder it, and to wonder how he got from there to here. Reverend Fox's voice slowly faded back into my consciousness.

"… and I remember young Martin when he turned eighteen. He eagerly went down to the Butler recruiting office and signed up to serve in the army. He wanted nothing more than to be like his father, who spent several years in the Pacific during World War II. The day after Martin signed up for the army, Maggie Kinney came to the church to pray. I remember I was fixing some molding around the window, and she asked if she could pray at the altar. She said that Martin had joined the army, and she wanted to say a prayer of blessing over him. She knelt down and prayed for a while, and then came over to me and said something I'll never forget. She told me that she knew that war was going to change Martin, but she asked God to forgive him for the mistakes that he would make. She looked at me and said, 'Pastor, I know that God will forgive everyone who asks for forgiveness. But can he also forgive those who don't have enough sense to ask for forgiveness?' I didn't know how to respond. I was still so young. Then she asked me if I would pray for Martin. I assured her that I would. I gave her my word, and I'm ashamed to say that I didn't keep my promise very well."

Reverend Fox paused and wiped a stray tear from his eye. *Why is he crying,* I thought. It didn't make sense. Was he shedding a tear for my dad? For lost opportunity? For admitting pastoral neglect? Then I thought of my grandmother Maggie. She loved the boy in the picture very much. How strange it felt to think this. I never knew my grandmother, and of course my dad never told me anything about her. It began to dawn on me that Vietnam changed everything about my father.

"Well, the Vietnam era changed us all," Reverend Fox continued. "Martin's life drifted away from church after he returned from Vietnam. But I wouldn't judge him too harshly. On the contrary, he's a hero. He served our great nation with distinction and honor. He willingly went when many others tried to shirk the draft by running to Canada or burning their draft cards. God loved Martin J. Kinney, and I'm here today to ask God's blessing on Jane and Martin Jr. as they grieve the loss of their beloved husband and father."

Without warning, Mom stood up abruptly, walked right up in front of the podium, pointed her finger directly at Reverend Fox and yelled, "Fornicator."

Complete silence. Nobody dared move an inch. Eternity elapsed within a matter of seconds. Reverend Fox stood frozen. Embarrassment would not begin to describe the depths of insanity that ran through my family. Nobody could make a scene like a Kinney. I knew my mother must be completely crazy. Without saying another word, she marched down the aisle with her heels reverberating loudly off the high ceiling. Soft whispers and murmurs added to the echoed chorus of her shoes. Everyone buzzed with excitement except me and Reverend Fox. I was angry and ashamed. It didn't make any sense. She was out of her mind. The hum of the small crowd continued to fill the sanctuary as my mom slammed the front door and left. Reverend Fox looked distraught, but quickly gathered his thoughts and tried to reassure the crowd.

"It's okay, everyone. Funerals are a particularly stressful time in everyone's life. We must not let the disruption obscure the reason for us being here – to honor Martin J. Kinney. I would like to ask Mrs. Grassley to come and play a closing hymn for us and then I'll offer a prayer of benediction."

My mother accused a man of God of being a 'fornicator' during the middle of her husband's funeral. I was baffled, yet not surprised. I had no desire to chase after my mother, so I stood and gave lip-service to the hymn that I had never sung before. Of course, I didn't really know what a hymn was. For the present, it was just a filler of time between when I would leave my dad's funeral and have to face my mother again. So in any case, I kept hoping Mrs. Grassley would play all six verses.

To Hanoi

Tan, my taxi driver, wouldn't let it go.

"Don't put wallet in back pocket. You shouldn't do that."

"I know."

We left Thai Nguyen as I continued to lament the fact that it was nowhere in the proximity of Tay Nguyen. I felt sick, yet hungry. The only thing I had to eat in this whirlwind of a day when I arrived in Vietnam was a bowl of noodle soup with raw pieces of beef in it, but that was well before the lake or the spilt ashes or the lost wallet or the laughing policemen. This trip had quickly turned into a disaster. I am a Kinney. What else should I have expected?

"You still have passport, right?"

"Yes," I replied to the nosy driver, who as best as I could remember was my only friend in the entire world.

"Is it in your back pocket?"

"No!"

"But you lost all your money? And credit card?"

"Yes!"

Tan befriended me in some strange way. I had paid him up front for a full day's drive, but he must have felt sorry for me. He dragged me everywhere and told me about everything, but nothing sank in. I languished in a foreign land, constantly thinking about my dad's last wish that I had completely messed up. I looked at Tan and saw a friendly guy with a wiry mustache and several black whiskers on his chin. Standing flat in his black dress shoes, he came up past my shoulder only a little – probably no more than five foot six and weighing a slim one twenty. It seemed strange to want to call a man dainty, but that description fit best. I was twice the man he was, well at least physically.

"So what you going to do?"

"I don't know."

"Okay. I help you."

"No, no, it's okay."

"No, I help you. I have American friend."

"I just need to call my Mom back in America."

"But you have no money?"

"No."

"Okay. I help you. Yes, yes. I help you. My American friend help you. You know, my father soldier too. He fight many Americans – kill many Americans – cause Vietnam don't like when America makes colony in Vietnam."

I tried to ignore him.

"We fight Chinese – make them leave many times. We fight French. Make them leave. Then Americans. We fight Americans make them leave. But don't worry. I love Americans. I have American friend. I take you there."

As my driver droned on about Vietnam's past, I couldn't help but picture the wind carrying my dad's ashes all over the heart of communist Vietnam. What a way to honor him! But, in fact, I was not honoring him. Not really. What was I actually doing here? Why was I so eager to fulfill this request? If dad had told me his story about the girl and Newbert and Johnson in his will, would I have jumped at the chance? Hardly. His voice. The sound of his voice enticed me, brought me close, and gave me a glimpse of how it might have been between us.

We had been driving for nearly an hour and a half when we finally glimpsed Hanoi from the top of a bridge over a river.

"This is Song Hong, Red River. And we go over Thang Long Bridge. Built by Russians. You know, America bomb us, but Russia build us bridge. But okay, I like Americans. In the past, I had to study Russian at form two. I hate studying Russian. Nobody wants to speak Russian. Everyone wants to speak English."

At least I had a friend.

"This bridge – Thang Long Bridge. You know what it means? Ascending Dragon Bridge. Long time ago, Hanoi not called Hanoi. It called Thang Long. Ascending Dragon. You know why?"

I frankly didn't care why.

"Why?"

"Because Vietnam emperor travelled along Red River and suddenly a mighty dragon comes out of the river and flies into the sky. So he called this place 'Ascending Dragon' and he made this his new capital. Now almost one thousand years, Hanoi be capital of Vietnam."

The river looked muddy – muddy like a flooded B52 hole in a rice paddy. How anything good could rise out of such a filthy, muddy stretch of water I would never know.

We weaved through the chaotic streets of Hanoi with our taxi often being a stranded, motionless island surrounded by a constant stream of motorbikes, which flowed haphazardly on all sides. I missed my Lyndora streets. Tan continued his lecture on the historical significance of every intersection and building and temple that we passed. After another twenty minutes, we pulled over in front of a large complex of buildings fronted by a massive metal gate.

"My friend here. Foreign Language University. He teaches English. Come. He help you."

I got out of the taxi and walked behind Tan up to the guard house. Tan spoke quickly to the guard who barked out some instructions and let us in. We walked past two four story, mustard yellow classroom blocks which had open windows with wood shutters tied back. Tan taught me all about the Vietnamese education system, but my mind didn't wander far from the banana trees or the crowded festival with the girl in white.

"He's right here."

We walked up to a modest looking two story cement guest house painted yellow. Everything seemed to be painted mustard yellow in this country. Tan knocked on the first wooden door and after a few seconds a young, trim, white American peaked out with an eager smile.

"Tan. How are you doing? I haven't seen you in a while."

"Hello Mr. Jason. I'd like you to meet another American."

"Hi," Jason reached out to shake my hand.

"Hi," I said. "I'm Martin."

"Hi, Martin. Good to meet you."

"Martin had his wallet stolen in Thai Nguyen. Now he has no money. He had it in his back pocket. I told him he shouldn't keep it there."

"I'm sorry to trouble you," I said feeling quite embarrassed. "Tan insisted that we come to visit you."

"Oh yeah, no problem, man. Come on in. What can I do to help? That really stinks. You do have to be careful around here. Lots of thievery. I used to have this large plant outside, and one morning I came out and someone had climbed over the gate and tried to steal the whole potted plant. But it must have been too heavy, so they dug out the plant instead and left a big hole in the pot's dirt. Whatever is not nailed down will be stolen around here."

He paused. I tried to look sympathetic, but I hoped he saw a difference in significance between losing my wallet and a kidnapped plant.

"Yes," Tan agreed. "Lots of young people using drugs. They need drug money. It's terrible."

"How can I help you Martin?" Jason asked.

"Is there any way that I could call America? I need to get in contact with my mom so she can wire me some money."

"Oh, sure. I can set you up on my computer."

"I don't want to trouble you."

"No, no trouble at all. It's dirt cheap. Come on in."

Within minutes I was sitting on the edge of his bed looking at a laptop computer screen which sat on the coffee table in front of me. Jason assumed at first that I knew what I was doing, which I didn't. He soon caught on that I was computer illiterate and helped me type in my phone number, put on the headset, and told me to wait for someone to answer.

"It's ringing," I said.

Tan and Jason went over to a small couch and sat down. Jason started cutting some bright purple tropical fruit as they chatted.

"Hello," mom answered.

"Mom, it's Martin."

"Martin, where are you calling from? It's six in the morning."

"Mom, I'm still in Vietnam. I need some help."

"What did you do? You get lost? Do you even know where you are? And what exactly are you doing there anyway?"

"Mom, listen. My wallet was stolen."

"Martin, you imbecile. Why did you have to run off across the ocean anyhow? You are such a fool."

"Mom, can you just listen? I need you to wire some money to me."

"You go against my wishes and have your father cremated, then you betray me by having his funeral in a church, then you run off around the world spending what little money your father left on some crazy scheme you dreamed up. You do all that without considering my feelings once, but now you have a problem and come running home to Mom. I'm tired of it Martin. You want to be grown up? You want to do things your own way? Well do it! I'm not sending you anything. You can figure it out yourself if you are so smart."

"Mom—"

She hung up. I sat quietly for a moment until I realized that Jason had walked over behind the computer.

"Hey, I'm sorry."

"No, it's just… my mother. It's complicated."

"Let me help you."

"No. It's okay. I appreciate you allowing me to make the call."

"No really. I want to help. What do you need? You still have your passport, right?"

"Yes."

"And how long are you staying?"

"I fly out the day after tomorrow."

"So you need a place to stay for two nights, some food, money for airport tax, and transport to airport."

"Yes, but," I tried to stop him but he continued to overwhelm me with hospitality.

"No I insist. You can stay here if you don't mind sleeping on the couch. Food is not a problem, and I am happy to give you some cash for the airport."

"That is really kind of you, but—"

"And don't worry about airport. I can take you. I go out there every morning looking for passengers," Tan added.

Their kindness overwhelmed me. I was a complete stranger with nothing to offer them, yet they willingly offered everything to me while my own mother turned me away in ridicule.

"Thank you. Thank you."

Perhaps I would make it home after all.

Reverend Fox

Reverend Fox bit his upper lip, then motioned for me to sit down on the leather couch in his study. He was reluctant to speak, but I could tell he wanted to answer my question if only the right words would come.

On the Monday after the funeral, I felt very unsettled about what had transpired. Mom hadn't spoken a word to me since she stormed out of the church after saying that inflammatory word. It didn't make sense, so I decided to visit Reverend Fox to see if he could enlighten me. I also wanted to thank him for his kind gestures during the funeral. In fact, my mother's blow-up was the only hitch of the entire funeral service. Not bad at all.

And so I sat staring back, waiting for a reply from Reverend Fox. He must have been in his early seventies, and he had a very kind, sincere face.

"Martin, some things in life can never be erased, at least not completely. They can't be undone, and they can never be forgotten. However, they also aren't meant to cripple you. They aren't meant to hold you back or stop you from moving forward. And so as you grow and change and hopefully learn some lessons along the way, you become a better person who isn't quite as likely to make the same mistakes you did as a youth. That's the theory at least. And while I believe all of what I said is true, sometimes the pain you have caused – even long ago – is still there."

I wasn't quite sure I followed. I was the least theoretical person I knew. One has no time to ponder theories when living in the midst of a hurricane. But I nodded out of politeness.

"Okay. Thank you, Reverend for all of your help with the funeral. You've been very nice to us, and I'm sorry that my mother acted the way she did."

I stood up and turned toward the door when Reverend Fox cleared his throat.

"It's true. Your mother was talking about me. When I was the young assistant pastor here, before she married your father, I had an intimate relationship with her."

"What? With who?"

"With your mother."

I gazed back, a frozen sculpture unable to think or move. Reverend Fox added to the silence perhaps not knowing what else to say. He said enough for a simple minded person like me to spend a lifetime thinking about all the ramifications of his revelation.

"You had a relationship with my mother?"

"Yes."

This certainly explained a lot, and I was sure that it explained things that I could not even comprehend.

"Martin, please sit down."

I sat and remained quiet. If I was a true Kinney, I would be yelling obscenities right about now. I might have even hit him. But sitting was all I could do. I could sit and be quiet like the best of them. I could endure any torrent of abuse, any gale of ill weather, any ridiculous situation by just sitting and remaining quiet.

"Martin, I'm sorry. I never intentioned to burden you with this knowledge, but after meeting you and seeing the relationship you have with your mother, I –"

He stopped and rubbed his eyes.

"Martin, you're a good son. I can see the goodness in you. I believe you endured a lot, but all you had on your mind when you came to me the first time was to honor your father, someone who was difficult to love. Someone who was embittered by the past. I was part of that past, your mother's and father's past. What I'm about to tell you has long since passed from my consciousness. I've paid for my sins, and I know that I've been forgiven. So I made it a point of not going around the rest of my life beating myself up for the mistakes I made in my youth. But this funeral brought home another important point; the consequences of one's actions may never fully be realized. Some people can't forgive, can't get over the bitterness and it eats them alive turning them into something much less than they were intended to be. So I feel obligated to you, Martin, to set the record straight. Do you want to know the full story?"

I nodded. Last Tuesday night I was a bowler. On Wednesday, my dad talked to me like a son, gave me a mission and breathed his last breath. Thursday, I stood up against my mother and arranged the funeral. Saturday, I received a picture of my father singing at church. Sunday, the funeral home gave me my dad's ashes. And now on Monday, I was being confronted with the foreign past of my parents. The narrow view I held of them completely shattered before my own eyes – my dad and a smiling Vietnamese girl – and my mom and a young assistant pastor. Life was simpler as a bowler. Eating spicy tacos and downing Cherry Coke at the bowling alley with my K-Mart team made me happy. I loved Tuesdays, but it now seemed that I would never face another normal Tuesday the rest of my life. And for some reason, I felt okay with that. I eagerly waited for more revelations from Reverend Fox. It was all so sordid, yet splendid. I felt alive. I felt important.

"As I said at the funeral, I arrived here in 1960. I was twenty-one years old and just out of seminary. Reverend Coonsley was the senior pastor, and he took me under his wings and set me to work right away doing various different duties for the church and congregation. One of my main tasks was working with the youth. That's how I got to know your father who was only ten years old when I came. Your dad consistently served in whatever capacity he was asked. He ushered during the Sunday evening service. He volunteered to hoist the flag every Sunday morning. After church, I would often help him re-fold the flag into a perfectly tight little triangle. Over the years, we became close, and I suppose it would be fair to say that he came to look up to me as a big brother. Those were good years. I learned a lot about service and faith and... well, all that doesn't really matter."

He leaned back in his office chair.

"Now, of course you know that your mother is two years older than your dad. Your dad met her in town one day. He was seventeen. She attended the local business school. She planned on taking a two year course in office related work. Your dad worked weekends over at Stevenson's Feed Supply – that place is long gone. Your mom took up an internship in the office there a few hours a week to practice what she had been learning at school. Did your parents ever talk to you about how they met?"

"No. Never. Not one single word," I said marveling at the tale he weaved.

"So they started dating and were together for about a year when your dad finally decided to join the army and go to Vietnam and fight. I admired your dad a great deal for how he got your mom involved in the church. Now as far as I know, your mom didn't come from a church going background. That didn't deter your father. Actually, he insisted that she come to church with him and his mom, and she did so very faithfully. She loved kids and started helping with the youth. She was great. She taught them songs that she had only recently learned herself. She quizzed them over their memory verses during Sunday school. So they were both very involved in church and with each other. This was right around the time of the Tet offensive in Vietnam. The war created a huge amount of division in the country. Did you ever learn about the Tet offensive?"

I wanted to say 'yes', but I had no idea what he was talking about.

"No."

"Tet is what the Vietnamese call their New Year. On the eve of Vietnam's largest celebration, the Viet Cong launched coordinated attacks against more than forty different targets all throughout South Vietnam. The coverage that came through on TV made everything look chaotic. Our government had been continually telling us that our soldiers were winning the war. They had daily casualty counts that told us how many VC had died the previous day. But then suddenly, the VC pulled off these coordinated attacks – even in the capital of Saigon where we supposedly had everything under control. After this, the public's attitude soured bitterly over Vietnam. It looked like a quagmire with no end in sight. People were just tired of it and became unsure of why we were even fighting. The summer of 1968 was horrible. The war protests, the assassination of Martin Luther King Jr., the race riots, the assassination of Robert Kennedy – the whole country was angry, upset, and unsettled. This really troubled your dad as it did all of us. He graduated from high school in June that year, and he resolved to join the army. He thought the war protesters were unpatriotic, and he felt the ultimate way of showing his support for his country was to join the armed forces – like your grandfather."

"I know my grandfather fought in WWII, but other than that I don't really know anything about him."

"I'm afraid I can't help you there," said Reverend Fox. "However, I do think your dad felt compelled to follow in his father's footsteps. Your mother tried to talk him out of it; she was very distraught about his decision. She came to me and asked if I would step in and try to get him to change his mind. But there was nothing I could have said. So he left for basic training at Fort Polk, Louisiana around September of 1968. Nothing would ever be the same after that date."

Reverend Fox looked tired. He stared off into space for a moment, and then reconnected with me.

"Martin, can I get you a cup of coffee?"

"No, thank you," I replied, just wanting to get back to the story.

Reverend Fox walked over to the coffee maker in the corner, poured himself a cup, then continued to divulge the past I never knew.

"Over the next several months, your mom kept abreast of your dad's whereabouts and doings as much as possible. When he shipped to Vietnam in early January of '69, your mom came to see me. She told me all about the last conversation she had with him, and then she broke down crying. I tried my best to comfort her. Over the first six months of 1969, your mom and I became good friends. I acted as her confidant about her feelings over your dad and everything she felt concerning his deployment. And for me, your mom was a great help at church. She devoted herself to the youth group, coming every Friday night, playing games with the kids and teaching Bible stories. I greatly admired her, and frankly, I grew fond of her. She was an attractive young woman – simply pretty and very pleasant to talk with."

What tall-tales he seemed to be creating! If he hadn't been a man of the cloth, I might have called him a liar. His words added depth and clarity to my being. I no longer felt like a one dimensional person continually on the receiving end of taunts and jabs and abuse. In a wonderfully strange way, I somehow knew that the web my parents had weaved over me was not real because the parents I knew were not real. They were merely just some beaten down version of who they used to be. I began to realize that Reverend Fox's story would not hurt me, no matter which direction it sprinted. I had, perhaps, already tasted the worst of my life.

"By the time the summer of 1969 rolled around, your mom stopped hearing from your dad. It was very upsetting for her, and we talked frequently about him. I told her not to give up on him, that war was sure to take a toll on him, and that we needed to keep praying for him. Your grandmother Maggie would pray for Martin every Wednesday evening at prayer meeting. She was such a faithful saint. She, too, took a good liking to your mom, and your mom and I would often spend Friday nights at Maggie's house eating dinner, talking, and wishing Martin safety."

The Reverend seemed taken in by himself. He gazed off for a moment.

"It was, I believe, mid-June. Your mom and I were in charge of a mini-youth retreat at one of the campsites up north near Tionesta along the Allegheny River. We had with us about 10 kids aged from twelve to sixteen. We all drove up together in the church van and set-up our tents in a campsite which jutted right out into the river, a beautiful little setting. Friday night and Saturday we did all kinds of activities with the kids – canoeing, tug-a-war, water fights, fishing. Late Saturday night, oh, it must have been after midnight, all the kids were asleep. I was sitting on a mat overlooking the river; the weather was brisk; lightening bugs lit up the night canvas like Christmas lights and the crickets and the frogs were out in full force. I heard someone coming. It was your mom. She sat down silently beside me for a while. We chatted nonchalantly about the beauty of the sights and sounds. She then brought up Martin, and said something about her being afraid for him. It was quite dark, and I had trouble seeing the expression on her face clearly. I reached out to give her a little pat of encouragement on her back, and I missed her back and touched her face instead. That single touch on that one night….well….it was one of those touches that get your heart racing. She curled her face in towards my hand, and— Well, remember I was nearly twenty-nine at the time. It had been a long time since I had a girlfriend. I truly was focused on my work at the church. But I certainly was not immune to the magical charms of nature. I then reached and pulled her close to me, and I hugged her with my right arm. She scooted over next to me and put her head in close to mine. My, I remember it like it was yesterday. I turned to Jane and said, 'Jane, I have a tremendous desire to kiss you. May I?' 'Yes', she replied. And we started kissing. Now you might think that since I was a pastor that I would have had better sense than to be starting something like this during a youth outing. I'm no more immune to mistakes than anyone, and so I pressed my luck, and we became more physical. Before you know it, I had led your Mom back into my tent, and we were intimate with each other."

He stopped. His heart seemed to race, and his eyes glazed over in some sort of nostalgic trance.

"She went back to her tent before morning, and the next day we could barely look at each other. I became obsessed with her. She flooded my thoughts every moment of the day. The next week, I couldn't concentrate on anything. I couldn't look Reverend Coonsley in the eye, I couldn't prepare my Sunday School lessons, and I couldn't pray. She consumed me. I thought for sure I was in love. I finally called her on Friday evening and said I wanted to see her, and we met at the Hot Dog Shop over in Butler. I told her I was sorry for what happened, and that it was wrong for me to not be able to control myself. She didn't say anything, and then I told her that I loved her. I couldn't help loving her. I didn't want to take advantage of her or complicate things with Martin. If she didn't want to see me anymore, I would understand. She then stopped me and said that she didn't want to stop seeing me. I had the biggest lump in my throat. And that was the start of the two most selfish months in my whole life."

I must have had a strange look on my face because Reverend Fox stopped and asked, "Martin, do you want me to continue this?"

"I do," I said forcefully.

"Well, for the better part of the summer of 1969, your mother and I saw each other on a regular basis. They were truly the most self-centered moments of my life because I said to myself constantly, 'I know I'm not supposed to be doing this. I know it is wrong of me to have an intimate relationship with her. I know that it will cost me everything that I've worked for and everything that I have learned about God. But I don't care. I want her more than anything else.' Martin, I basically said, 'Damn the consequences, I'm doing what I want to do.' By August, everything in my life was unraveling. I couldn't keep up with my work at the church. The youth activities had slacked off to nothing at all. I avoided your grandmother like the plague. I found myself lying to Reverend Coonsley about the silliest things just to cover up any inkling about our relationship. And I completely blotted out your father's memory from my life as I think your mom tried to do as well. Finally, by mid-August, I was such a wreck that one evening I went into Reverend Coonsley' study and confessed everything. I wept on the floor waiting for hell-fire and brimstone; waiting for God's damnation to shake every bone in my body. But the most amazing thing happened; Reverend Coonsley got down on his knees, pulled me to himself, hugged me and prayed something so simple yet so powerful that I will never forget it. He said, 'Lord God, show brother Daniel how much You love him. Show him how much You love him.'"

Reverend Fox had tears streaming down his face.

"That night changed me forever. The power of that prayer, the power of love, the power of forgiveness overwhelmed me. I was no longer the same. He told me to go home and read the Prodigal Son and then come back in the morning, so we could talk about the next step. I went home and read the Prodigal Son about five times. No matter how I tried to think about it, I could do nothing except receive God's forgiveness. Every time I read the story, the father welcomed home the wayward son with open arms. I finally began to understand God's love. The next morning, I met with Reverend Coonsley and we talked through the entire story. I knew for myself, for your mother, for your father, and for your grandmother that our relationship was wrong and that I needed to break it off. Later that day, I brought Jane back to Reverend Coonsley, and we went through everything. We all agreed that the relationship would end, and I told them that I would leave the church. But in the meantime, the church elders had met to discuss discipline. They recommended that I be put on a two year probation period and had direct supervision into my relationships and interactions with people. I grew tremendously in my faith over those next two years, and I learned that I couldn't let my mistakes keep me from doing what God had purposed for my life. We all make mistakes. Some bigger than others, but we still must move on."

"How did my Mom deal with the break-up?"

"Not so well. She stopped going to church, and I didn't see her at all for a number of months. Once I ran into her over at Rexall Drugs, but it was one of those awkward-don't say anything kind of moments. I didn't really understand what I did to her until more than a year later when your dad returned from Vietnam. One day I heard that Martin had just returned home. I really wanted to go see him, but of course part of me was very reluctant. But I had to, so I went over to your house there on Home Avenue and Martin was on the front porch. He looked completely changed. He had his tattoos on his arms, he was smoking a cigarette, and his eyes just floated around like he wasn't completely coherent. We chatted briefly about different things, and I remember before I left that I told him I hoped to see him in church; he just smiled and went into the house. About four days later, it happened. I was at home in my little apartment above the garage of the parsonage. I heard a car pull up out front and a car door slam. Then I heard the heavy pounding of footsteps up the wooden staircase, and a loud thud of a knock on my door.   I opened it up and there was your dad. He was very drunk, and he had hate written all over him. He immediately started yelling at me about how I had slept with his girl, and he threatened me. Finally, he punched me in the face, and I fell backwards onto the floor. He lunged at me and pinned me down while beating me with both fists. I finally broke away from him, but he, in his drunken rage, relentlessly went after me. He turned over my coffee table, and threw two lamps onto the floor, the whole time yelling curses and threats at the top of his lungs. I truly was frightened. The whole neighborhood lit up. The Perkins were standing on their front porch across the street. Reverend Coonsley showed up, and when he couldn't get your dad to settle down, finally yelled to the Perkins to call the police. Your dad kept up his tantrum for another five minutes and then finally went back down the stairs and got into his car. Just as he backed out, the squad car pulled up and your dad had another incident, this time with the police. They arrested him for disorderly conduct and let him sleep it off in jail overnight. Of course, I never pressed charges, but they warned Martin to stay away from me. Your dad never came back to church. Maggie was right. The war changed him tremendously, and of course my actions toward his girl just reinforced his doubts about life, faith, and God. Your grandmother Maggie stopped going to our church after that as well. She started attending one over on Main Street in Butler. I believe she did it out of respect for her son, who struggled to come to grips with what I had done. Your dad never did start going to church again anywhere. About two months after that, I saw in the Butler Eagle that your mom and dad had eloped. I never talked with them again – ever. When I spoke to your mother at the funeral, it was the first time in nearly thirty years. I would run into Maggie from time to time and we would chat about how they were doing. She always seemed very concerned for them. Maggie passed away in '73 when you were only…"

"A year old," I said.

Reverend Fox nodded.

"Maggie was quick to show me a picture of her

grandson that's for sure. So, Martin, I can't speak for your parents or for the type of upbringing you experienced. I can only relay to you of what I knew of them. Your dad walked away from his faith because of Vietnam and because of me, and I don't know what else. Your mother and I experienced a very painful relationship which put a tremendous strain on her relationship with your dad. And then, of course, she had to cope with being with a person who had changed greatly due to the scars of war. No doubt, the foundation they built their marriage on was rocky at best. But I guess they stuck with it, and stuck together with each other all these years."

I certainly didn't want to speculate with the Reverend about why my parent's marriage did last all those years. I couldn't even begin to guess why.

"Martin, I don't know if that long rambling story will help you or not, but I felt it important for you to know the truth. I'm sorry if I caused your family undue pain and suffering. It was never my intent. And I truly meant what I said about your father at the funeral. He will always be a hero to me."

"Thank you, Reverend Fox. Your story means a lot to me. I'm really glad you were willing to be part of my dad's funeral."

I stood up, shook his hand, and left the parsonage. As I got to the front sidewalk, I glanced over my right shoulder and saw the garage and the apartment with its white rising wooden staircase. It was all too easy to imagine my dad making a scene, yelling, cursing, and getting arrested. That part seemed normal. What I couldn't imagine was my mother as a young woman sneaking into that apartment to spend the night with

Reverend Fox.

The brisk air sent a shiver up my spine. *Very appropriate*, I thought.

On My Way

My mother was never much of a drinker. But for the two days immediately following the disastrous funeral, she kept a bottle of bourbon within arm's reach. I stayed out of her way, and we exchanged very little except glances over those next forty eight hours. They say that when a person is missing that the first forty eight hours is the most crucial. I know this wasn't the same situation, but I wondered if I should have tried to talk with her. I wondered if I should try and step in to make sure she wasn't disappearing; however, every time I thought about her or dad or Reverend Fox or their relationship, my mind went blank and my body went numb.

After the funeral when I brought the urn home, she looked at me with daggers in her eyes.

"Get that thing out of my house. Why did you think I wanted him buried? I wanted him out of this house for good."

I didn't say anything about the cremation or Vietnam or my intended trip. I just took the urn into my room and hid it out of sight.

Three days after the funeral I went to AAA to look into flights to Vietnam. I told the travel agent I needed to go to 'Tie Win' and after she looked up a few things told me I needed to fly into the capital. I told her I wanted to go as soon as possible but that I only wanted to stay for no more than two days.

"Are you sure? That's a long and expensive way to go for only two days," she asked with a look of uncertainty on her face.

"Well, how far is Tie Win from the capital?"

"Well, see here. It is spelled T-H-A-I-N-G-U-Y-E-N," she said pointing on the map of Southeast Asia. "It's right here. So using the scale, it can't be more than fifty miles outside the capital."

"Then two days is all I need."

I had no intention of sightseeing. I had only one mission in mind and that was to fulfill dad's wish. Besides, I knew absolutely nothing of Vietnam. I'd never met a Vietnamese person in my life, and I was pretty sure that I wouldn't want to eat their food.

"There is a flight this Friday. You'd arrive in Hanoi on Sunday morning, fly back out on Tuesday night and so you'd arrive back in Pittsburgh on Wednesday morning. It's $2200."

"It's perfect."

"Now, I can work on getting you an expedited visa on arrival. And, of course, you do have your passport already, right?"

"Yes."

I actually did have a passport. In July 2001, one of my buddies from work got this bright idea to fly to Puerto Rico for a vacation. He was really into classic drag racing at that time, and he heard on TV that the world championship was being held in September at the Salinas Speedway in Puerto Rico. After much pleading, he convinced me to go with him. So we both sent away for our passports only to find out later that Puerto Rico was a part of the United States and that we didn't even need them. To further rub salt in the wounds, we never got to go because our September 15th flight was cancelled because of the attacks on the World Trade Center days earlier. My timing was always impeccable and my knowledge always overflowing.

I had $3000 in my savings account which had taken me about ten years to accumulate, but I intended to spend it all on dad. I plopped down the cash which I had withdrawn earlier in the morning, and ten minutes later I walked out to my car holding in my hands the itinerary to Vietnam.

I felt nervous and worked up. I couldn't believe I was actually going through with this; now all I had to do was break the news to Mom.

I bottled up the explosive news for two more days, but on Wednesday morning I sat down beside her as she ate her breakfast of cereal and toast.

"Mom, I have to talk to you about something."

She looked up at me for a moment and then continued eating.

"Dad asked me," I stopped and stumbled over my words. "Dad…"

"Martin, just say it," she snapped in her snarky way.

"Before Dad died, he asked me to do something for him."

"Martin, what foolishness are you talking about? If I could just get you to shut up about your father."

"Mom, listen. Dad told me he wanted to be cremated, and that he wanted his ashes to be dumped out in Vietnam."

"Martin, what are you talking about? Vietnam? Vietnam? That place destroyed him. That place destroyed his life. He came back from Vietnam, and I didn't recognize him."

"Mom, but that was his wish."

"Why, Martin? Why? Why would he have said such a foolish thing as that? You never could understand anything we told you. Why are you so stupid? Stop talking about Vietnam."

Browbeaten, yes. But not knocked down. I knew resolve previously unknown.

"No, I won't," I barked in a forceful tone. I had bought my ticket, and I was going no matter what. Her words couldn't stop me now. "He told me a story, and..."

"Oh no," my Mom interrupted. "Not the girl? The girl story? Really? Is that what this is about?"

"Well..."

"Well, is it or not? The girl story. The beautiful girl in the white flowing dress that unrobed for him under the banana trees?"

She knew the girl story. I couldn't believe it.

"Well, yeah, he did tell me a story about a girl."

"How many times did that drunkard tell me about the beautiful girl he had his way with under the banana trees. The biggest piece of BS in the world. So just drop this whole ridiculous thing. Just drop it. I don't want to hear another word of it."

But Mom wasn't there on his deathbed the night before he passed. Mom didn't hear the sincerity, didn't see the tears, didn't hear the pleading. I felt bad for her that he would have ever told her that story. She didn't deserve that nor did she deserve what Vietnam did to her husband. But I couldn't change any of it. I couldn't change his drinking rage, his belittling nature, or his crass talk about women. But I could fulfill his dying wish, which I intended to do even if it upset my mother. I had to do it.

"Mom, I know you aren't going to like this. But listen to me. Honestly, I hated Dad. I loathed being around him. I hated everything about him – how he treated me – how he treated you. But on his deathbed, he was a different person. He talked to me for the first time like I was a man, like I was his son. And for the first time ever, he asked something of me. He wasn't asking it out of his overwhelming need to belittle me and dominate me. He asked me out of humility because he needed my help. And I promised him that I would do it for him."

"Promise," my Mom said with disgust. "He never kept a promise in his life. Why should you care about a promise to him?"

"Because I'm not like him," I said bluntly. "I refuse to be like him."

I looked down at the tile for a minute. I had tears in my eyes. I just wanted to scream; I felt like the house was condemned and ready to collapse in around me. I never felt so smothered in all my life, but I was also never this determined.

"I will keep my promise. I leave for Vietnam on Friday."

I turned and walked out of the kitchen.

"Do whatever the hell you want," she yelled after me.

I would. I designated Thursday as the day to pack, and

the first order of business was to figure out how to transport the ashes. I didn't want to be separated from dad, so I thought I would need to carry it onto the plane. I got a two quart Rubbermaid container from the kitchen and thought that it would have to do. I hoped beyond anything that dad was no more than two quarts, even though that seemed like a very morbid thought. I put the plastic container on my bed and went into my closet, peered through my shirts to the small shelf hidden in the back where I had hid the urn. I carried it to my bed, opened the lid and stared intently at the grey fine ash. Then I poured the contents into the Rubbermaid; it filled up the whole container with just a little left over, which I left in the urn and put back on the shelf. Careful not to spill any ashes, I put the lid back on the container, sealed the whole thing with grey duct tape and placed it in my backpack. My carry-on was set.

Hanoi

"Excuse me, sir. Congratulations on eating the whole rack of ribs. For doing so, you get a free pint of beer," said the thin Vietnamese waitress holding a glazed over mug topped with a frothy head.

"Oh, that's nice. But I'm sorry, I don't drink beer," I said and looked over at Jason. "Jason?"

"Oh, no. Not me. My teaching organization forbids it, though I'm sure Tan can help us out and make sure it doesn't go to waste."

Tan grinned widely and reached out his hand.

"I'm happy to help," he said as he took the beer and immediately began guzzling.

Jason and Tan were phenomenal friends to me. Maybe it was the rumbling of my stomach or my eyes which constantly wandered over to Jason's stash of snacks, but one way or another they knew they needed to feed me. And that they did. They took me to one of Hanoi's popular western restaurants and ordered me a whole rack of ribs. I must admit it hit the spot more than the green leafy grass and soup Tan got for me after we had left the police station in Thai Nguyen. After I downed the massive ribs, the heaping fries and four Cokes, my stomach purred beautifully. First time I felt full in three days due to travel and my country-side escapades. I didn't know how to thank my gracious, accidental hosts. I felt indebted, but when I tried to thank them, they seemed almost embarrassed by my flattery.

After Tan finished the beer, we walked into the busy, broad avenue and the street lights greeted us as dusk closed in. Cars and motorbikes whizzed by at dizzying speeds, but Tan and Jason helped me dodge them effortlessly as we walked north for a block towards the glittering lights which illuminated the trees around Hanoi's most famous lake.

"This is Hoan Kiem Lake," Tan continued his history lesson. "It means Returned Sword Lake. There is a famous story about a giant turtle that lives in lake. One day the emperor ..."

Tan talked as he always did. Jason asked clarifying questions about the story, and as I listened half-heartedly, I came to realize that I had been in Vietnam for nearly twelve hours but I had yet to experience or see Vietnam. My whole focus had been on fulfilling my dad's wish, of which I had failed miserably. But now, for the first time, I began to look at Vietnam around me. This was certainly not the Vietnam that my dad experienced. But there was something vibrant about it. It had something that Lyndora did not – life. We crossed the street and started walking around the edge of the lake. People were everywhere doing everything. A group of old men sat under a lamp post playing Chinese chess. A steady stream of joggers weaved their way through the commotion. A group of boys carrying wooden boxes approached every foreigner asking if they wanted a shoe shine. Couples snuggled close on benches gazing at the lake, perhaps hoping for a turtle sighting. Sellers balanced a scale-like bamboo contraption over their shoulders hawking exotic fruit and fresh baked baguettes while others sold toothbrushes, toiletries, and toothpicks.   One small boy tagged along with our threesome halfway around the lake imploring us to buy a pack of Wrigley's gum off of him. The chaos overwhelmed my senses, and I became entranced by the ceaseless action and the unrelenting flow of people. Every few seconds I saw that girl, the one I had clung on to, the one who stole from me, the one with the innocent face and the smooth skin. The one that nearly smiled at me. There she went again, and again. Every thin face, every curved body, every long haired girl looked identical to her. I wished the girl, whom I had held in my tight grip, had smiled at me. What would I have done? My dad knew what to do when a girl smiled at him. I was not like my dad.

Magical. My heart stood squarely in a magical place. I could feel the swelling of my hands and the lump in my throat. *This is Vietnam. This is where my dad left his soul. This is where the girl smiled at him. This is where my dad will remain forever.*

"Martin, you gotta try this place out. Best ice cream in the world. Come on."

We crossed over the double lane, tree lined avenue and entered a small French ice cream shop tastefully decorated with black metal, curved chairs and small round, wooden tables. We chatted about nothing in particular as Jason ordered several different flavors for us to sample. I was particularly interested in the young women who sat mainly in small groups sharing a common sundae. They all looked so familiar. The raspberry sorbet lit up my mouth with such a bright, smooth and cold flavor that I quickly admitted that it was the best I had ever had. I had never thought about what I would find when I came to Vietnam because I treated this trip as my mission – nothing more. But in the matter of a few short hours, I had met some of my best friends, sampled some of the best ribs, licked some of the smoothest ice cream, and watched some of the prettiest girls. As we left the ice cream shop, the lights in the trees and from the buildings danced on the water.

"How you like Hanoi the capital?" asked Tan.

"It's amazing," I concluded.

"Tomorrow, I take you to some places in Hanoi, so you can see more, okay?"

"Sure. Anything you like."

I had one more day to experience everything my dad never did.

American Soldiers in the North

The policemen at the station in Thai Nguyen did not tell the precise truth. They laughed at the prospect of American troops in the north during the war, and I played the part of the ignoramus for even suggesting my dad had served around Thai Nguyen. However, I learned that there were some American soldiers in the north during the war, just not in the capacity that I had envisioned.

Early the next morning, Tan picked me up at Jason's university to take me around Hanoi on my last day in Vietnam. We first stopped for some breakfast when I sheepishly reminded him that I still didn't have any money. He ordered two large bowls of "pho" with that same raw beef that I stared in horror at the day before. But this time, the onions, spices, and subtle chili flavor brought my taste buds alive. I dunked the raw pieces of beef in the piping hot soup and managed to slurp down my noodles using the ceramic spoon with quite a bit of enthusiasm. Life was different now compared with yesterday and so were the noodles.

Our first stop after breakfast was the flower village,

which he excitedly told me had the wreckage of a B52 bomber. Sure enough, as he pulled off to the side of a small square lake surrounded by typical two and three story Vietnamese homes, rising out of the water stood the metal wreckage of a B52.

"Everyone calls this B52 Lake. We shot down the Americans and the plane crashed here, but the pilots all survived. Parachuted out. All of them captured and taken to Hoa Lo prison. We go there later," said Tan. "You have camera? I can take picture for you."

I didn't even have a camera. I came here in such a rush that I really hadn't thought through anything. I only wanted to comfort dad, which I hadn't. I still felt sick about the ashes under the wrong banana tree.

I walked around the small pond looking intently at the three airplane tires still halfway jutting out of the water. They must have been sitting that way for more than forty years. The irony of it all seemed palpable. A B52 bomber is swallowed up by a lake, yet all the airmen survive. A single soldier jumps into a rice paddy only to be drowned in a hole left by a B52. I wondered if Johnson floated to the top after a while; perhaps his backpack stuck straight out of the water like the B52 wreckage. Perhaps the sole of his boots glimpsed the light of day like the airplane's tires sat suspended over the murky water.   I envisioned my dad hanging on to the side of the rice paddy thinking about his dead friend just feet away.

"Lots of American pilots shot down around here," Tan woke me out of my trance. "You don't have a camera?"

"No."

"That stolen too?"

"No."

"How come you spend so much money to come to Vietnam but only spend two days and don't bring a camera?"

"There was something I had to do."

"I know. You had to find banana trees by a lake in Tay Nguyen," Tan laughed. I didn't think it was particularly funny. "I never understand Americans. I like Americans. I do. Mr. Jason, he's a good friend of mine. But sometimes I don't understand him. On Tet New Year, he comes to my house for a meal, but he shows up wearing short pants and shirt with no sleeve. Very strange. That's clothes for sleeping not for visiting. How come you don't wear short pants? All Americans wear short pants. Maybe you are too fat," he answered his own question.

I had to keep reminding myself how grateful I was for Tan.

"Let's go. Nothing more to see here. We will go to Ba Dinh Square. Only one kilometer from here."

As I turned to walk back to the taxi, two sprawling trees ablaze with the color red stood staring back at me.

"What kind of tree is this?" I asked.

"Oh, this is the *Phuong* tree. *Phuong* tree one of the most beautiful trees in Vietnam. Many girls have name Phuong too. In English, we call it 'flame tree'."

"It does look like it is on fire. Very beautiful."

"Just like Vietnamese women. On fire, and beautiful," he started laughing uncontrollably. "What you think of Vietnamese women? You have a girlfriend?"

"No, I don't have a girlfriend."

"You should meet a Vietnamese girl. You want a Vietnamese girl?"

"No. I'm leaving Vietnam tomorrow."

"Why you don't want Vietnamese girl? Lots of Vietnamese girls like American men."

"Even American men who have no money?"

Tan started laughing uncontrollably again.

"That's right. You have no money. No chance to get Vietnamese girl. Vietnamese mothers okay with daughter marrying American man if he has money. But no money, no chance, especially someone big and fat like you," he smiles and breaks off a small branch of the Phuong tree. "Here. This is a symbol of a Vietnamese girl you could have had if you had money."

I took the flaming red flower of the *Phuong* tree and put it into my shirt pocket as the only Vietnamese souvenir I could afford. Then we hopped into the car and began once again driving down the narrow streets dodging animals, bicycles, three wheeled trishaws, swarms of motorbikes and other cars which continually beeped their horns for no discernible reason.

Ba Dinh Square revealed itself in an obvious way. I felt like the square's expanse could have contained all of Lyndora. The massive open air square was divvied up into small sections of grass separated by cement sidewalks. Next to the vast lawn was a very broad avenue which authorities had permanently blocked to all motorized traffic. On the other side of the avenue stood the tallest structure in the square – the granite columned mausoleum of Vietnam's beloved 'Uncle Ho' – Ho Chi Minh. Ho, who had died of natural causes in 1969 during the Vietnam War, was permanently preserved – lying in state in a Sleeping Beauty-like glass case placed in a dimly lit chamber guarded by stoic soldiers. His skin looked pale and wax-like. The whole experience of standing in line and walking in a single file, silent parade past the body of the one who led them to freedom from the French, kind of creeped me out. It felt good to emerge from the darkness back into the sunshine. As we reached the other end of the square, we stopped to overlook the immense French built, mustard colored presidential palace.

"Ba Dinh Square is the most famous square in Vietnam. It was right over by the mausoleum on September 2, 1945 that Uncle Ho stood up and declared our independence from the French. And you know, he borrowed the first line of the American Declaration of Independence to also be the first line of Vietnam's Declaration of Independence."

"Really? Is that true?"

"Yes. 'All men are created equal and endowed by their Creator with certain unalienable rights.'"

"Really? That's true? I never heard that before."

"Yes. That's true. Ho Chi Minh liked Americans. You know that day on September 2, 1945, there are American soldiers here too, in the crowd, listening to him declare independence. You see, two months earlier, American soldiers parachuted into Vietnam and trained Ho Chi Minh's soldiers so they could better fight against the Japanese. American soldiers right here."

Another piece of trivia I never learned at Butler High.

"You know something else. No one likes to talk about this, but it's true. You know in Ho Chi Minh's will, he wanted to be cremated. He didn't want to have a mausoleum. He didn't want to be preserved. No, he wanted to be cremated, and he wanted his ashes divided into three and spread out in each part of Vietnam – north, central, south."

I couldn't help but think that maybe I should have done that to dad. Divided the ashes in three and dumped them in each region of Vietnam just to cover all the bases. But no. I had to accidently spill them over a thousand miles away from his intended resting place.

My mother and Lyndora had nearly faded from my consciousness. I lived history. I understood American history more in two hours with a Vietnamese taxi driver than I did spending year after year sitting through social studies classes at Butler High.

By 1 PM, we had visited the B52 site, Ba Dinh Square, Uncle Ho's House on Stilts, the famed One Pillar Pagoda and the Ho Chi Minh Museum. Tan then treated me to *Bun Cha* – a famous Hanoi dish of charcoal grilled strips of pork in a spicy vinegar sauce with rice noodles. The twelve hour time zone difference really hit me after lunch, so I napped in the back seat of Tan's taxi while he slept in the front seat enjoying his normal mid-day siesta.

I dreamt I was back at the banana tree and I had the ashes in the Rubbermaid container. From behind one of the banana tree branches stood a Vietnamese girl wearing a conical hat and a long flowing white *ao dai* – their traditional long dress with pants underneath. I cocked my head to the side to see her face. She moved slightly, and I could tell she smiled at me. I wanted to get closer, but I held the ashes. I needed to do something with the ashes. She smiled again and waved for me to come. Her face was pale – almost ghostly white. Her skin had no blemishes. Her beauty drew me, and I wanted to be with her, but the ashes wouldn't let me leave. So I quickly opened the red lid of the container and dumped them on the ground right next to me. As I took two steps toward the girl, I quickly looked back, and I had this sinking feeling that something was terribly wrong. Those were not my dad's ashes. No. They were not my dad's ashes. 'Mom', I said looking at the pile of ashes on the ground. Then I remembered the girl and turned back towards her, but she was gone.

Tan jiggled my belly back and forth.

"Martin. Wake up. Time to go to prison."

I rubbed my eyes and shook off the bizarre feeling the dream left me in.

"Here. See here? This is Hoa Lo prison."

Tall mustard yellow cement walls stood about fifteen feet tall right out my taxi window. The tops of the wall were sprinkled with colored broken glass and several strings of barbed wire. In the background, a large modern skyscraper dwarfed the prison.

"During the war with the Americans, the American soldiers called this the 'Hanoi Hilton'. But this prison not important to us because of that. This prison held many, many patriots who fought in the war of Independence from the French. Come. We see."

We walked through the arched doorway and came to the ticket seller who expected me to dish over the equivalent of three U.S. dollars to get in. However, Tan did some quick talking, supposedly about how I had no money. She eventually smiled, then laughed. The joke was obviously on me again.

"Come on. It's okay," Tan finally said and we entered into the dimly lit, grim prison chambers. Tan told me all about the heroic efforts of the Vietnamese political prisoners who escaped and constantly lived under threat of death. Death in this prison was by guillotine, which was still on display in one of the larger rooms.

"Many Vietnamese patriots lost their heads here. But their cause was not lost. When we became independent from the French, all Vietnamese – both living and dead – rejoiced greatly. We all like to be free."

"You're right," I said as I looked over the long list of Vietnamese martyrs listed on the wall next to the guillotine.

"That's why it seem so strange when America comes to fight in Vietnam. We know America is the land of the free. Statue of Liberty. We only wanted to be free too – like America."

I paused for a moment and wondered how to respond.

"Well, sometimes we perceive things differently from one another."

I sensed he didn't know what the word *perceive* meant.

"My dad. He came to Vietnam because he thought he was doing the right thing. He wanted to serve his country and promote freedom. But—"

"Did he like Vietnam?" Tan asked.

"He had a terrible experience in Vietnam. It changed his whole life."

"So your dad didn't like Vietnam?"

"Only the women," I smiled at Tan.

"Yes, Vietnamese women very beautiful. But you broke, remember," Tan said as he burst out laughing again.

As we entered one of the last rooms of the prison, we finally met the American soldiers. On the walls were pictures of many of the prisoners of war who had been captured in North Vietnam and collectively served many years at the Hanoi Hilton. There were pictures of the soldiers attending mass at the Catholic Church. There were pictures of the soldiers cleaning a turkey getting ready to celebrate American Thanksgiving. There were pictures of soldiers at rest and soldiers at play. It was a wonderful display of propaganda meant to show how well the American prisoners were treated.

"See. American soldiers treated real well here. Real well," Tan said.

"So, all of these pictures are true?" I asked being a little skeptical.

"Of course. We love Americans."

The Trip Home

I was wide awake at 2 A.M. still on Lyndora time. Jason slept silently in his bed as I gazed at the ceiling from his sofa trying to take everything in. I dreaded going home and I loathed thinking about what life at home after dad would be like. In a strange way, I felt closer to dad now than I had since I was a boy. I thought about the photo of him and me at Conneaut Lake, and then I thought about the time we spent together at Nui Coc Lake in Thai Nguyen. Even though I miscalculated by a thousand miles, the connection felt remarkably strong. What would mom be like without dad to provoke her? Would she soften in her widowhood or had I already driven her into an embittered state by dragging up old wounds and going against her wishes? I wondered how my life would ever go back to normal, and if I actually wanted it to. I couldn't imagine showing up at the stockroom with much enthusiasm. The thought of unloading hand mixers, TVs, gardening soil, and boxes of Tylenol seemed absurd. Is that what my life had really become? The world in Vietnam seemed so vibrant and alive, and I a mere hollow shell drifting back and forth between my couch, my work, my bed, and my bowling alley. *What a waste my life has been,* I thought. *How could I go back to that house? Maybe I could move? Maybe I could get my own apartment? How about a new job?* These thoughts flew in and out of my mind for hours as I kept replaying the last week and a half while trying to anticipate what the future had in store for me – a fatherless Martin Kinney Jr. I half-laughed out loud when I thought of the word fatherless – like I ever had a father to begin with.

I dozed in and out for the next four hours and finally got out of bed at six. Tan was to be there at 6:15 to take me to the airport. After I came out of the bathroom, Jason was sitting on the edge of the bed.

"Hey, morning. You ready to take off?"

"I guess so. Oh, and I'm sorry to tell you this," I started to confess. "But when I sat on your toilet, the seat broke. I'm really sorry."

Jason started laughing.

"I can't even take a crap right these days."

Jason rolled in laughter then chimed in, "Don't worry about it. These Vietnamese bathrooms are hardly meant for Americans. Those toilet seats are about as sturdy as a saltine. But I'm sure these little Vietnamese butts could sit on a saltine without cracking it." He smiled and handed me an envelope. "I mean, you did notice the shower head, right? Metal fixture coming right out of the wall at a height of around five feet five. I have to hunch over just to get my hair wet."

His easy going attitude made me laugh, and I reached for the envelope.

"What's this?"

"You are going to need a little cash."

"No, no, you've been—"

"Martin. You need to pay the airport tax to get out of the country. Then you need a little cash for food or whatever."

"But—"

"Martin, it's okay. It's my pleasure to help you. Really."

"I don't know what to say. You've been really kind to me. I don't know what I would have done without you."

"Tan told me about your father's death and what you tried to do for him. I really respect that. I know it's been a tough week for you, so I'm glad I could make it a little better."

"Thank you," I said, appreciative of a level of kindness I never experienced in my own home. "I hope to come back to Vietnam someday. I was just starting to experience it."

"You should do that, and let me know when you are coming." He looked down at his watch. "It's almost 6:15. Tan will be waiting outside the main gate. We should go."

Tan wasn't there. While we waited Jason bought me a small plastic bag filled with sticky rice, shaved pork and fried onions. I devoured it in about three bites.

At 6:40, Tan arrived in his white and blue taxi apologizing for being late because of his breakfast. But he assured me that we would make it to the airport on time. I thanked Jason again for his kindness and we drove off, dodging a rapid river of motorcycles every inch of the way. After about twenty minutes of nudging our way through traffic, we entered the highway and before I knew it we were crossing that same Thang Long Bridge exiting the city. The Red River did have a tinge of red to its muddy water. I glanced back once to see the mass of cement houses of Hanoi surrounded by a smattering of high rises in each direction. Another fifteen minutes and we passed the toll booth and came to the final cross roads; straight went to the airport; on the right side of the road stood a green road sign "Thai Nguyen 50KM". I thought of dad, and immediately my breathing picked up and I had a nervous twinge right through my stomach and a small swelling of tears in my eyes. *He's so far away. He'll be so far away forever,* was the only thing I could think. I started to second guess myself. *Should I have really have brought his remains here? Why didn't I just listen to Mom? He's an American veteran who had his ashes poured in the heartland of communist Vietnam.* Tan mumbled non-stop about various English questions to which I only grunted in reply. He answered all his own questions anyways so it didn't matter.

"Here you go, Mr. Martin."

"Tan, thank you so much for all of your help. I learned so much about Vietnam, and I couldn't have survived without you."

"You're welcome Mr. Martin. You write me an email, okay?"

"When I get a computer, I will. And I'll pay you back for all your taxi rides."

"No, no, no. It's okay."

I nodded in appreciation again and then walked into Noi Bai Airport in search of my flight home. I flew from Hanoi to Bangkok to Tokyo to Los Angeles. Twenty seven hours including layovers. I kept wondering what I would find when I got home. On the flight to Bangkok I sat between two scrawny Vietnamese men. They both reminded me of Tan, as they talked non-stop to each other right over top of me. My large frame did nothing to impede them. My flights were a frightening and uncomfortable time of anticipation. I was lonely. I missed my two-day old friends, and I missed Hanoi. On the long flight to LA from Tokyo, I sat next to a Catholic priest who was returning to San Diego from a youth conference in the Philippines. We talked civilly on and off throughout the flight. At one point the conversation turned to religion.

"Do you believe in God?" he asked.

I thought fast. I really didn't want to get into it.

"I was just in church last week," I said slickly.

For some reason that response satisfied him. I shuddered in horror to think of him probing deeper along those lines. I don't think I could have told this story at that point.

When we landed at LAX, everyone was herded into the immigration lines. I followed the crowd feeling incredibly out of place. When my turn came, I approached the immigration officer who stood behind a counter with a computer screen in front of him.

"Can I have your passport?"

"Oh, yes," I said nervously and reached into the front pocket of my jeans – the same jeans that had lost the wallet out of the back pocket – and handed it to him.

"Where are you coming from, sir?"

"Tokyo."

"How long were you in Tokyo?"

"Just two hours."

"Where did you come from before that?"

"Bangkok."

"How long were you in Thailand?"

"Just two hours."

The officer at this point looked up at me and had a perturbed look on his face.

"Mr. Kinney. What I'm getting at is where were you spending your time overseas? I'm not asking about your layovers."

"Sorry. I was in Vietnam."

"And how long were you in Vietnam."

"Two days."

"And what other countries have you visited," he persisted.

"None."

"So you went from the United States to Vietnam and stayed only two days? Is that right?"

"Yes."

"Why such a short stay?" he inquired.

I was starting to get nervous. My whole life sounded like a joke.

"Well, I was just going there, and I," I said stumbling over my words and the officer glanced right at me.

"What were you doing in Vietnam, Mr. Kinney?" he said in a more forceful way.

"I was burying my father."

He raised his head and gave me a startled look.

"Well, no, I wasn't burying him. I just brought his ashes to Vietnam. He asked me to take his ashes to Vietnam."

"You are carrying ashes with you now?"

"No, no. I dumped them out. They are in Vietnam under a banana tree. Not that that was important."

"Why were you bringing your father's ashes to

Vietnam?"

"He asked me on his deathbed if I would bring his ashes there. You see, there was this girl, and, well, actually he was a soldier in Vietnam during the war and, and, he was very sick, and he asked me, after he told me about the girl that smiled at him, ah, then..."

"Mr. Kinney," the officer interrupted my rambling. "What do you do for a living?"

I stopped and looked squarely at him.

"I work in the stockroom of K-Mart in Lyndora, Pennsylvania, sir."

He sized me up again, looked down at the passport and chopped it once.

"Thank you Mr. Kinney," he said and pointed toward the baggage claim area.

I breathed a sigh of relief. My country wanted me after all. I had felt like an unwanted orphan during that short exchange. Another bout of humiliation – a sure sign I was getting close to home.

I took the red-eye to Pittsburgh landing at 5:35 AM. I felt so tired and hungry. I had used all the money Jason had given me, and I only hoped that my stockroom colleague remembered to pick me up. If not, I would be stranded thirty miles from home. The airport transit train unloaded me at the air mall. I walked past the statue of the young George Washington who surveyed the back hills of Western Pennsylvania as a young British officer. I imagined Tan as an American taxi driver telling me all about the young George – I missed him. It dawned on me that George and Uncle Ho of Vietnam had a few things in common – the great symbol of freedom for their people. George stood beside the other great symbol of our region

— a statue of Franco Harris making the immaculate reception. I'm sure Tan would have had no equivalent for Franco.

I descended to the baggage claim area and found my conveyor number on the display board. Belt 1. As I approached the belt, I looked and then looked again. I thought my jet lag played tricks on my eyes. Standing in front of me, arms calmly at her side, slight smile on her face stood my mother.

"Hello Martin. Welcome back."

She spoke with a warm, unfamiliar glow. Her face seemed calm without a hint of anger or frustration.

"Mom?"

"Welcome home," she said and came over to give me hug.

My tongue locked. My heart nearly stopped. My stomach ached and twirled.

"Mom?"

I could say nothing else.

"I'm glad you're home. Let's just put all this stuff behind us and live our normal lives. Okay?"

"Okay."

Emotion welled up in me. Tears slipped slowly down my cheeks. She met me at the airport. She didn't yell at me, and above all she hugged me. I hadn't felt a loving touch from a parent in such a long time. I had trouble putting my emotions into perspective the whole ride home. We said very little to each other except for a few exchanges about how the airplane rides were. She asked me nothing at all about Vietnam or dad's ashes, and I certainly didn't feel that I could bring any of it up. Perhaps it all didn't matter anymore. Perhaps just these few days apart put everything into perspective for her. Maybe it wouldn't be like it used to be. Perhaps we could finally put the abusive past behind us and slowly pretend to be family. It's strange that during the entire two days travel home I could think of nothing but Vietnam, my new friends, the girl who stole my wallet, the lovers cuddling by Turtle Lake, and the ashes under the wrong banana tree. But now, Vietnam suddenly seemed less important – a mere distraction from everything that was really important in my life. Could it be that my excursion abroad would bring us together? I started missing my room at home; even the thought of showing up to work at K-Mart didn't seem too bad. *It will be fun to bowl with my buddies on Tuesday,* I thought. I looked out the window as the sun rose, a red ball. Its piercing light blinded me, and I eagerly awaited what this new day would bring.

Three Years

I slept for fourteen hours. I awoke around 10 PM and started unpacking my suitcase. There wasn't much to unpack since I didn't buy any souvenirs. As I threw my clothes into a pile on the floor that would eventually end up in the laundry basket, I remembered something about my blue striped button down shirt. It was the shirt I wore when Tan took me sightseeing around Hanoi. I reached into the front pocket and felt it immediately – the Phuong tree flower petal. It was still brilliant red in the shape of fan with a serrated edge. I laughed when I thought of how Tan told me it represented the girl that got away because I didn't have money. It made me think about dad. I traded my dad's ashes for a red flower petal. I touched it gently and smelled the faint sweet scent emanating from it. I went into the dark living room. *Mom must have already gone to bed,* I thought as I turned on the stand lamp and walked to our book shelf built into the wall and encased with wooden framed glass doors. I opened the shelf doors and looked for a book in which to place the petal. After glancing through the shelves, one particularly large hard cover picture book caught my eye – *A Day in the Life of Vietnam.* I had never seen it before. I removed it from the shelf, went into my bedroom, and spent the next hour pouring over each photograph until I saw her on page 89. It was that same Vietnamese girl with the simple smile, the small statured frame, who looked taller due to her thin features. It was that girl that popped into my sights on every street corner, at the ice cream shop, and in dad's dreams. It was most likely the same girl that sat on the rock in the banana tree grove looking down at my father. This girl, too, had a smile on her face. I stared at her for several minutes and then pressed the Phuong flower petal directly against her and closed the book firmly. I placed it on the night stand and lay back down in bed. I would be back at work in the morning.

I settled back into Lyndora life. Mom and I lived civilly, not completely unlike before; though without dad, the house had lost a lot of its edge. I continued unloading coffee makers, particle board furniture, and electronics from the eighteen wheelers which rolled into the loading dock on a daily basis. On Tuesdays, I bowled with my gang and continued to eat those spicy tacos. Sunday afternoons were filled with NASCAR.

I ran into Reverend Fox over in Butler about six weeks later. We chatted briefly, and I told him an abbreviated version of my Vietnam trip. I told him my mission was accomplished, and I thanked him again for his help. In nearly every way, my life went back to normal. I thought less and less about dad as time went on, and I guess I could have said the same thing about my trip to Vietnam. I did from time to time skim through the pictures of the Vietnam picture book, and I always stopped to rub my fingers up and down on the red flower of page 89.

Three years passed from the date of my dad's death. Lyndora and I continued as usual sauntering slowly towards twilight unaware of what stood just beyond the horizon. I never could have anticipated what I was to find in front of my house on Home Avenue in Lyndora one late spring evening. Perhaps I was not the same person after all.

Part II

I am My Phuong.

Point of Contact

He stood as wide as a bus – a target too easy to spot and easier still to nail. I had been pickpocketing for several years, and foreigners were the easiest and typically most rewarding prey. On festival days, I always wore my all white *ao dai* which made me seem more dainty and lady-like. I was always told I had an innocent looking face, which I also exploited as an important asset.

This one stood tall and wide, and completely out of his element. Hung walked beside me as usual. He had a very intense look on his face. The crowd pressed thick on this overcast day that was pleasantly cool. We walked deliberately, wading through the festival goers toward the target. We pressed and pushed. He wore jeans which made everything that much easier. Hung now walked directly behind the tall, red-headed foreigner or *tay* as we called him. I walked just behind him to his right watching the varied movements of his backside as he jaunted through the throngs. Hung glanced quickly and nodded; then I counted to three. Exactly on the three-count, Hung put two hands on the giant's back and violently pushed

him forward. He nearly toppled an old lady in front of him.
A split second after the push, my hand, which had been
placed on his behind at the count of two, quickly slid in
and out of his back pocket clasping the wallet. I quickly slid
the wallet up the left slit of my *ao dai* and into my
underwear. I then pushed past him to the right while Hung
split past him to the left. Someone grabbed my left wrist
and squeezed. The large foreigner pulled me hard toward
himself as the festival goers continued proceeding
intermittently and haphazardly like stalled rush hour
traffic. I glanced at my captor and looked directly into the
face of the large red-headed beast. Foreigners, at times,
seemed more like specimens than humans. He had
scraggly red hair on his face and arms with round ruddy
cheeks.

"Where is my wallet?" he yelled at me.

Hung got away, but I had the goods. I stared at him
pleading mercy with my eyes. Would he notice my
innocent face and my beautiful *ao dai*? How could I be a
thief? I tried to wriggle free, but he had a very firm grip. I
resolved to stare him down. My eyes were watering,
asking him *Why? Why are you being so cruel to me? Why
did you grab me? You are hurting me.* He looked away
from me but continued his firm hold. But I knew he was
wavering, for I saw the doubt in his eyes. He looked to his
left and then right. He seemed unsure. He didn't know if
he had the right person. He looked once more into my
eyes, and I felt his fingers release their grip one by one. I
turned, head down, and tried to put some distance
between me and *tay*, who was so kind to leave his wallet
in such an accessible position.

I learned never to run from a scene. I also had

learned if no one in the general vicinity of the incident got a good look at what happened, then it was often a good idea to stick around. No one ever suspects a nicely dressed young woman loitering around a crime scene to be the culprit.

About ten meters down, I forced myself through the crowd and into the temple courtyard, which sat on a small bank overlooking the main strip. I watched the tall, red-headed foreigner from behind the courtyard's metal gate. He kept looking in every direction. He was agitated and so very out of place. I almost felt bad for him. He seemed to have no friend in the world, and now he had no money. I thought it was silly to feel bad for him because after all, he was a rich foreigner. After another minute, he was out of sight. I would now go and meet up with Hung and see how we did.

———————

Eight hundred and twenty one American dollars. It was a good haul. I skimmed a hundred off the top and put it in my bra as I waited for Hung to show up at the small boarding room he rented off the backend of the university. I was surprised to beat him here. His loss. I kept the rest of the money in the wallet but looked through everything else. A credit card, an insurance card; then I pulled out his driver's license.

"Martin J. Kinney. You have a fat face. Where are you from? 1201 Home Avenue, Lyndora. You are a long way from home Martin. But I thank you for your kindness, and I thank you for putting your wallet so conveniently in your back pocket."

I heard a motorbike pull into the courtyard. It was Hung. I slide the license into my bra with the money, and threw the wallet onto his bed. He entered and closed the door behind him.

"Well, how did we do?"

"See for yourself."

"You didn't look, did you?"

"No. You know I would never do that."

He went to the bed and opened the wallet and counted it out.

"Seven hundred twenty one."

"Good," I said. "Now give me my share."

"I'll give you three hundred."

"You'll give me half."

"Hey, I'm running this operation."

"I do the hard work. Anybody can push someone from the back. Give me three hundred and sixty dollars."

Hung talked tough, but I wasn't afraid of him. I wasn't really afraid of anybody. I've been battered, beaten, and bruised enough to know when I should back down from a threat. But Hung was nobody. I knew he would give me the money, and he did. I headed towards the door.

"Tomorrow?" he asked.

"No, I'm working tomorrow."

"But that's the last day of the festival."

"I don't care. This is enough to last me while."

He came towards me and grabbed my arm.

"I want to do it again, tomorrow."

"Then you'll be doing it yourself. I'm busy."

I yanked my arm free and left.

I had been renting a couple of rooms with my friend Hoa off the back courtyard of a house that belonged to a local university teacher.   A teacher's house lends an aura of respectability that we tried to maintain. I took off my *ao dai* and removed the items from my bra. The license caught my attention again. He had such a funny looking face. His face was as wide as three Vietnamese faces. I couldn't help but think what Martin was doing right at that moment. How would he cope with losing his wallet? What would he do? How would he get home? I don't think it was remorse creeping in, but I did have a sense that I certainly would hate to lose my wallet in a foreign country. But of course, I knew better than to keep it in my back pocket.

"Thank you Martin! Four hundred and sixty dollars. A very good day."

I looked at his face another time, and then I went over to my friend's desk, took her hole-punch and punched a hole out of the left corner of his license. Then I attached it to my key chain.

"My good luck charm."

The Shave

When I first left home, I ended up spending many nights in dark places with strange men just trying to survive. It's the night society of Vietnam; the part that the communist cadres try to deny or ignore until something happens that makes it become too embarrassing. Then they raid a couple inconsequential karaoke bars for show. But that's what it is – show. Half the cadres themselves can be found in those dark places on most nights. The local police happily look the other way when presented with the right sized envelope. It's all about who you know and how much money you have. I was happy to leave that lifestyle, so when I got a chance to start cutting hair in a local salon, I took it. My friend Hoa, whom I met when taking some evening English lessons at the local university, introduced me to Co Thu, the owner of the only air conditioned, glass door salon in Thai Nguyen – a clear step above the 'hole in the wall' open air hair cutting places which dotted the main roads. Co Thu took a liking toward me and gave me a chance. So I worked in the salon about six days a week, but I still made time to freelance with

Hung from time to time.

One day after working there for about a month, I had to take on double the load because one of the other hairdressers was sick and didn't show up. A little after noon, a very well dressed gentleman with slightly greying hair, a handsome narrow face and a neatly trimmed, thin mustache, came into the shop. Co Thu jumped out of her chair to greet him, smiled unabashedly, bowed slightly and shook his hand. She talked to him in an animated fashion for a few moments then pointed towards the back, and he walked down the hallway and entered one of the private rooms. Co Thu quickly approached me.

"I need you to go cut that gentleman's hair – right now."

"But, I'm in the middle of—"

"Just go now," she said cutting me off.

"Yes, of course," I said as I put down the electric trimmer and scissors and walked down the hallway and into the room.

As I entered, I nodded slightly and went to organize the cutting tools which sat on the stainless steel tray on the counter next to the man. His eyes followed my every move, though he said nothing.

"Would you like a haircut?"

"Shave."

I reclined his chair back so he directly faced the ceiling. I wet my hands and gently rubbed his cheeks with warm water. He barely even needed a shave since his skin felt rather smooth. I lathered the brush and put the shaving cream on his face.

"What's your name," he asked abruptly.

"My Phuong."

"You are not from around here," he said immediately recognizing my southern accent.

"No."

"What brought you to Thai Nguyen?"

"Work."

"Do you miss your family?"

I didn't want to talk about my family, so I ignored the question.

"Do you? Do you miss your family?" he repeated.

"They are dead."

"I'm sorry to hear that," he said in a sympathetic voice. "What happened to your family?"

"They died in a bus accident," I lied.

"Let me guess; the driver fell asleep at night?"

"Something like that."

"That's terrible. When did that happen?"

"About three years ago."

He stopped asking me questions as I used the straight razor down his cheek and around the curve of his jaw. He closed his eyes, occasionally opening them to look at me. When I finished shaving him, I rubbed his face with a towel, and then started soothing both of his temples with my fingers. I worked his face over gently massaging his facial features for about five minutes. Then I dug my fingernails into his scalp and began to itch his entire head. When I finished, I leaned over towards him.

"Would you like anything else besides a shave, sir?"

He opened his eyes and looked directly at me. He paused for a moment, and I felt a nervous twitch run through my stomach.

"No, just a shave."

He sat up and cocked his neck from side to side for a

moment. I handed him his suit jacket which he promptly put on as he stood up.   I had a very strange feeling about him. He carried himself well beyond the ordinary men who often came in here expecting something and exhibiting a condescending attitude. He had dignity – and it made me nervous. He reached for his wallet and handed me ten fifty thousand dong notes which was the equivalent of about twenty five dollars.

"Oh … no, sir. That is too much."

"It's hard to lose one's family. I'm sure a little extra money can be useful for you."

"No, no, I can't."

"Buy yourself a new outfit to go with that pretty face of yours."

The money clung to my hand, but I made no eager grab for it. I smiled softly and nodded timidly to show my appreciation. Then the man left. I started cleaning up the work station when Hoa burst in the room with wide eyes and a huge grin.

"What happened?"

"What do you mean?" I asked. "I gave him a shave."

"That's it? Just a shave?"

"Yes. What's the matter?"

The look on Hoa's face spoke of an unknown fact lingering on the horizon. I wondered if I would like what this revelation would reveal. I clearly missed something.

"That was Mr. Duc."

"So. I don't know a Mr. Duc."

"Mr. Duc. The head of Thai Nguyen's People's Council. He's the top official around here."

"Really?"

"Yes. So it was just a shave?"

"Yes," I said. "And he gave me 500,000 just for a shave."

"What? He gave you 500,000 for a shave. What else did you do?"

"I didn't do anything. Just a shave."

We bantered back and forth for a while about Mr. Duc. Hoa was so caught up in the whole incident, but I honestly didn't care. I'd been around too many politicians in my day to become too impressed with anyone — though I had to admit that he treated me quite kindly.

Co Thu didn't mention anything to me about giving Mr. Duc a shave. She just told me to get back to work when I came out front.

The day after I met Mr. Duc, Co Thu asked to meet me in the back after we closed the shop. I was surprised to see Hoa there too.

"My Phuong, sit down. I've noticed that many of my customers really admire your work."

I didn't say anything.

"Or maybe they really admire you. For example, Mr. Long, the banker, used to only come in here occasionally for a cut, but I think he's here twice a week for you to give him a shave and wash. That's a good thing. It's good to be liked by people. It's good to build relationships. You never know when they can be useful."

Co Thu was about forty-five years old. She was kind, but had an underhanded air about her. Her aging face didn't deter her from dressing in short skirts and tending to flaunt her womanhood in all the ways that attracted a gentleman's eye.

"I have some clients who are in the need of some delicate attention. There are occasional parties where they like to have some …"

She hesitated.

"… some hostesses to make the evening more enjoyable. Hoa sometimes goes to these sort of parties, and she thought that perhaps you would like to try it sometime."

Any girl who had spent time in those dark places knew what they were talking about. Most likely some sort of VIP get-together where secrets need to remain such. I looked at Hoa who was nearly expressionless.

"Now, My Phuong, Hoa told me that you spent two years in Karaoke clubs and rundown hotel rooms."

I looked at Hoa quickly rather surprised that she would share my secrets.

"I would never ask you to do something like that, but there are opportunities to be had – rather lucrative opportunities if one is not afraid. You are a very attractive young woman. You are independent. You are far from home. I think we understand each other."

I understood very well. What I wasn't sure of was if I actually had a choice in the matter. Co Thu had always treated me fairly, and I trusted Hoa for the most part, but I couldn't help but wonder if this was not a request. Would I be out of a job if I said no?

"So, would you like to give it a try?"

"Okay," I nodded.

Hoa smiled at me and took me by the hand.

"Good. There is a get-together Saturday evening. I'll have Hoa fill you in on some things. And why don't you take Saturday off from the salon. Meet me here around nine in the evening."

I nodded at her and left the room hand-in-hand with

Hoa. As we left, she told me everything.

My Former English Teacher

Before I got the job at Co Thu's salon, I had been working those seedy karaoke bars delivering drinks and satisfying selfish desires for nearly two years. I came to Thai Nguyen as a desperate soul. It was by chance, actually. I had travelled north on the train to Hanoi and had spent two weeks looking for some kind of work. I started pickpocketing by hanging out at the bus station. One day as I swiped a foreigner's wallet, I tripped and fell, and he had me pinned on the ground. I kneed him in the stomach as hard as I could. As he stood up to quench the pain, I rolled over and took off. I ran around the corner and right onto a bus that was just pulling out of the station. I jumped through three people who stood at the door and ducked down to hide. The bus took off, and I was gone. It travelled to Thai Nguyen, and I stayed there ever since. The small town feel suited me better. I was the exotic "flower" from the south and many guys were eager to have me. The men repulsed me, but I concentrated on nothing but the money since I had few other choices. I also found Thai Nguyen to be an exceptional place for petty theft. People were quick to trust and slow to catch on that I was out to get them.

But I never contented myself to lay on my back every night for strange men. I enrolled in a non-matriculating English night course at Thai Nguyen University. I had learned some English when I lived in the south, and I discovered I had a talent for it. My night job gave me plenty of money to pay the tuition, so I started a course under an American volunteer teacher who lived and worked at the university.

Sweet Miss Jessica lit up every room she entered. I adored her from the moment I met her. Her infectious smile and warm laugh welcomed me like no one had ever welcomed me before. She always had time to answer questions, and she seemed genuinely interested in getting to know me. I also had some of the best English abilities in the class, so we bonded together quite quickly and I spent many of my afternoons at Jessica's guest house laughing, learning, listening to music and just hanging out. Her place became my oasis – a place where I could forget what I did each night which remained a complete secret. I studied for two years under Miss Jessica and earned an advanced English certificate which I hoped would get me a better job. That was about the time that I was introduced to Co Thu and began to cut hair. I didn't have as much time to visit with Jessica during that third year in Thai Nguyen, but she would always be my number one friend for whom I would do anything.

When I got to my room the evening after giving a shave to Mr. Duc, Miss Jessica came to see me and asked if I would come with her in the morning and translate at the thirtieth anniversary ceremony of Thai Nguyen University.

Since Co Thu had given me the day off, I immediately told her that I would, so on Saturday morning I met Jessica at her guest house and escorted her to the ceremony.

Several hundred chairs were lined up outside in the courtyard in front of the administration building. The school's brass band mercilessly played only two off-key anthems as people found their seats and waited patiently for the dignitaries to arrive. Jessica and I sat about three rows back with many of the other esteemed teachers.

"What are they waiting for?" Jessica asked when the clock struck 8:30.

"Definitely a dignitary. Dignitaries always show up late. They must show up late, that way everyone can lavish their attention on them. If they came on time, it would be like making no entrance at all."

"That's really different from America. We start on time, and if the guests don't show up, well that's their fault."

"Vietnam is a patient country. We lived with the Chinese for a thousand years, but when we got the chance, we kicked the bastards out."

Jessica laughed.

"You're too funny. Where did you learn that lingo?"

"American movies," I replied.

"Well it feels like we have been waiting for a thousand years. Oh look, someone is coming."

A large black Nissan entered the main gate to the left and drove to within fifty meters of the podium. Out jumped three men in black suits. One I recognized immediately – it was Mr. Duc.

"I know him," I said to Jessica. "I met him yesterday in the salon. I gave him a shave. It's Mr. Duc. Head of the

Thai Nguyen's People's Council. My whole salon was buzzing from his visit yesterday."

"Really. You gave him a shave?"

"Yes. And he gave me 500,000 as a tip."

"Wow. That's pretty good."

Unfortunately, the band went into another rendition of the national anthem and everyone stood up and sang as the esteemed guests made their way to the platform. The ceremony consisted of an hour of pompous dignitaries spouting the party line about development, education, and building a better tomorrow for the people of Vietnam. It all rang hollow to me. I had seen and heard it all before, and it wiped my family out. I hated every one of those individuals on the platform, but I put on an excellent show for Jessica. I clapped vigorously at every introduction and stood solemnly at every appropriate time. I was such the patriot, though I continued to chat with Jessica during the speeches. Most of the time I spent watching Mr. Duc wondering why he gave me so much money. I wondered who shaved him this morning.

When the ceremony ended at about 9:45, the esteemed dignitaries came down from the platform and started greeting those in the first few rows. The university president singled out Jessica and had her come to the front. She grabbed my hand and pulled me in tow. Mr. Duc stood directly beside Rector Lieu.

"Mr. Duc. I want to introduce you to our foreign teacher. This is Miss Jessica Hanson. She is from New York."

"Miss Jessica," said Mr. Duc in English. "Thank you for coming to Vietnam and teaching English here. English is a very important part of our development. We greatly appreciate your service."

"I'm honored to meet you, sir. I love teaching in Vietnam. The people are so friendly."

"And how do you find the food?"

"It's incredible. I especially love *bun cha* and of course *pho.*

"Everyone loves *pho*", he said with a smile.

At that point, Mr. Duc looked past Jessica and right into my eyes. I smiled at him timidly, and he smiled back in a rather surprised manner.

"Is this a friend of yours?" he asked Jessica as he looked at me.

"Yes. This is my good friend My Phuong. She was my student for two years. She took night classes to earn an advanced English certificate. She is a very bright student."

"Hello sir," I said timidly and bowed my head slightly.

"So she is one of your star pupils?" Duc asked Jessica.

"She's the best I ever had."

"That's good to hear. I hope you enjoy your stay in Thai Nguyen."

"Thank you, sir," said Jessica.

Mr. Duc moved past Jessica and glanced once more my way. Our eyes met, and he smiled warmly at me. He intrigued me.

"Look at that. He asked all about you," Jessica boasted to me.

"No."

"Come on. He'll be back for another shave before you know it."

I did wonder if I would ever meet him again.

"Hey, are you busy now?" Jessica asked me.

"No. I have nothing going on until tonight."

"Great. Then come back with me to my guest house. I have some friends coming from Hanoi and we are going to barbeque this afternoon."

"All right," I said as I noticed Mr. Duc getting into his black car and driving away.

———————————

When we got back to Jessica's guest house, two Americans were waiting for us.

"I'm sorry. I hope you haven't been waiting long," Jessica apologized to the one male and one female who were sitting on the wicker patio furniture. They both looked to be in their early twenties.

"No, don't worry about it. We just got here about twenty minutes ago," said the girl who gave Jessica a hug.

"Hey, this is Vietnam. We're used to waiting," said the tall and quite handsome guy.

Jessica also gave him a quick hug.

"Sarah, Jason. I want you to meet my dear friend My Phuong."

We all greeted each other in a very friendly manner. One thing I admired about Americans was their friendliness. Every American I had ever met went out of their way to be kind and polite to me. They treated people casually – like you were long lost friends although you had just met each other. In typical fashion, I was laughing and jabbing away with Sarah and Jason in no time at all. I volunteered to take Sarah to the market to buy meat and vegetables while Jason worked on starting some charcoal which Jessica had piled high in an old pig trough. We were all fast friends.

When Sarah and I got back from the market, the

charred pieces of wood glowed a deep grey with brilliant orange around the edges. They put the large rack of ribs and the pieces of chicken on the grill as we chatted about what it was like for foreigners to live in Vietnam. I was always fascinated by this topic and wondered if I would ever get a chance to experience another culture.

By the time we sat down to eat, we had a veritable feast in front of us. Ribs, chicken, cole slaw, and cans of Pringles but no beer. Jessica and her friends never drank. They said their organization forbad it, which seemed bizarre to me. I loved beer, especially with barbequed meat. Vietnamese men have a social custom called *nhau* when friends will go out and drink, eat and socialize. Not to be restricted by social mores, Hoa and I would *nhau* at least once a week. At the end of the night we would stagger onto our motorbikes with red faces and little inhibition before hitting the night spots. But now I would have to settle for a Coke as they brought out several bottles from Jessica's room.

"Jessica, do you have a bottle opener?" asked Jason as he put the bottles of Coke on the fold-out table.

"Yeah. In my kitchen cabinet. Second drawer on the left."

"No need. I have one on my key chain," I said and pulled it out from my purse. I had a Hanoi Beer bottle opener right on my key chain which Hoa and I used liberally – never in front of Jessica though.

I handed Jason my keychain and he opened the bottles one by one and tossed the key chain down on the table. We chatted and laughed over the food and drink. It wasn't as happy as it would have been if they were beer drinkers, but we had a very good time overall.

At around 12:30, we were stuffed and Jessica and I settled down on her couch and crashed up against each other.

"I'm so full," I said.

"Me too," said Jessica. "Jason, just come and relax. We can clean that stuff up tomorrow."

Jason was outside piling up dishes and glasses on the table. Suddenly he entered the room with something in his hand.

"Is this yours?" he asked me pointing at the key ring in his hand.

"Yes."

"Martin Kinney. You have a driver's license for Martin Kinney. I know Martin Kinney."

A painful shot of adrenaline ran through my being. *That is impossible,* I thought. There is no way he could know Martin Kinney.

"I met him last week. You know Tan, right?" he asked Jessica.

"Sure, I remember Tan. He's the taxi driver that took us to see the pottery village."

"Yeah, that's right. Tan brought this guy to my guest house just last weekend. He had lost his wallet and was all out of sorts. I felt so bad for the guy. He came here to bury his dad's ashes who was a soldier during the war, and he lost his wallet and credit cards and everything. I gave him a place to stay for a couple nights and a little spending money so he could make it home."

My heart raced. Would my friends find out what kind of person I really was? After all, I had to admit to myself then and there that I was nothing more than an English speaking thief and former prostitute. My heart nearly exploded. Why was I like this? What brought me to this point of depravity? It certainly was not my upbringing. If my parents were alive, they would be so ashamed of me. At that point, I was so ashamed of myself. How could I face these fun-loving foreigners as nothing more than a thief? I didn't deserve their friendship.

"Where did you get this?" Jason asked the dreaded question.

I paused. I paused for an eternity – or so it felt. I didn't want to answer the question. Jessica sat up and had a concerned look on her face. What would I say? What could I say?

"Well," I started not knowing where my words would take me. "What a coincidence! Last week, I was over at the *Le Hoi Chua Hang* – the Chua Hang festival – and I had this stone in my shoe. So I stepped over behind the wall of the temple to see what the trouble was. And as I looked down, I saw a wallet. It seemed very strange to have a wallet there, so I opened it up and there was nothing in it except this American driver's license belonging to Martin Kinney. Of course, I had no idea who he was, but for some reason I kept the license. It's become my good luck charm."

They seemed to buy my story. I was always good at creating stories off the cuff. Jason looked down at the license again and shook his head.

"This guy was so far out of his element that I thought he was going to kiss me when I took him to Al's for a rack of ribs. But you know, he called his mom on my computer, and she just lit into him, swearing at him and telling him how stupid he was. Poor guy."

"Aww," sighed Sarah in sympathy.

I nervously fretted about what to say, but I was determined to keep up the façade.

"Now I feel so bad that he had so much trouble. The thief must have taken the money and then ditched the wallet. I can't believe that you actually met him. How strange!" I said convincingly.

"I know. What are the odds?" asked Jason.

"Well, do you want to send the license back to him? Do you think he would want it?" I asked trying to seem naive.

"Well, probably not. He's been home for a while now. I'm sure he is getting a replacement license."

"That's amazing that you both had something to do with this guy," said Jessica.

"Totally. It's kind of creepy," said Sarah. "Definitely hold onto that license. It's got to be a good luck charm."

I agreed. I would not let it out of my sight.

A Politician's Mistress

I survived the Martin Kinney Jr. driver's license incident. The thought of Jessica finding out my true nature took my energy away. I got home around three and just fell asleep for about three hours.   When I awoke at six, Hoa was there and she started going over everything I needed to know for the evening party. I needed to have my *ao dai* neatly pressed and ready to go. I felt very emotional and wondered how this night would end.

At 8:45 we got on our motorbikes and headed to the salon to meet with Co Thu. We entered to greet Co Thu who was on the phone. Hoa and I sat down and waited for her to finish.

"Yes," she said. "They'll be over shortly, and yes, I remember. It's all taken care of on my end."

She hung up the phone and looked at us.

"You two look beautiful. Are you all ready to have a good time tonight?"

We both nodded.

"Good. Hoa, it is not at the usual location tonight. Tonight it is at the 'Big House'."

Hoa looked surprised.

"You've been there once, right?"

"Yes."

"So you understand?"

"Yes," Hoa replied. "We will be fine."

"Okay. It's time for you to go."

Hoa nodded and took me by the hand and led me back out to the motorbikes.

"What is it?" I asked. "What is the 'Big House'?"

"Forget everything I told you. We are not going to one of those parties that I described at all. This will be a little more intimate."

"Intimate. With who?"

"I'm not sure."

"But you've been there before?"

"Once," Hoa said. "And..."

She stopped as she put her helmet on.

"And what?"

"We are going to the People's Council Guest House, and there is going to be a cadre waiting for us. It could be anyone."

"What's going to happen?"

"I don't know, but don't worry. When I was there last time, I ended up playing billiards with a deputy police chief all night. It was okay."

"And did he?" I looked at her trying to understand how far things went that night.

"It was rather innocent. He just kind of flirted with me, but nothing too serious."

"Did you ever see him again?"

"No."

"Do you think he'll be there tonight? And who do you

think I'll meet?"

"I have no idea."

Hoa pressed the automatic ignition button. I straddled my motorbike and did likewise.

"It's not far," Hoa said. "Just follow me."

We drove downtown past the city center and the market, which was boarded up and quiet. We passed the cinema which had a scarce crowd based on the number of vehicles out front. Then we pulled into the courtyard of a large old colonial house. The sign out front read "People's Council Guest House." I had spent many nights with many strangers, but for some reason I was nervous. I was used to men coming to me – coming to sing Karaoke and then asking for something more – coming to spend the night in a hotel only to spend the night with me. But this was different. I was no longer on my own turf, and I had no idea what to expect.

We both wore our traditional *ao dai*, and I must admit we were beautiful. We parked our motorbikes off to the left of the house and entered through the front door. A man dressed in a tux greeted us – it was the first time I ever saw a tux in Vietnam – and pointed us through the main doors into a large hall which was decorated with teak furniture with mother of pearl inlays. Only two men mingled about in the hall. They looked at us when we entered but kept their distance.

"Just be patient," said Hoa. "They'll come for us."

I felt nervous – almost sick in the stomach. I had turned away from this kind of lifestyle only to find myself once again in a high risk situation. We stood there silently, glancing every few seconds to the individuals who whispered in the corner. Finally, one of those men, a tall slender one who walked with his shoulders back and head held high, approached us.

"Miss My Phuong?"

"Yes."

"Right this way."

I glanced at Hoa, and she nudged me on with a soft push.

"It's okay," she said. "Go ahead."

He led me to the opposite end of the room, and up the staircase to the first room on the left at the top of the landing. I looked down to where Hoa stood, but she had already gone. I felt very much alone.

"Go on in," the man said and then turned and made his way back downstairs.

I slowly opened the door and walked into the large suite which was tastefully decorated with vibrant red and green colored paintings depicting various scenes of rural Vietnam. The room included a work space with a large wooden desk, a sitting area with a sofa, loveseat, coffee table, and a large bed with high wooden posts. On the opposite side of the suite stood a man in a business suit. He stared out the window and could only be seen from behind. He had black hair with strands of grey on the side. Closing the door behind me, I walked over to the sofa.

"Hello, sir."

The man turned around. It was Mr. Duc.

"Hello, My Phuong," he said.

My heart raced but my mind was blank.

"Please, sit down," he said as I sat on one end of the sofa and he came over and sat opposite me on the love seat. "It is very nice that I get to see you again. Maybe you are surprised?"

I nodded.

"The American teacher said you were her best English pupil ever, so your English must be very good."

I nodded.

"There is no need to be so formal My Phuong. I thought maybe we could be friends, and perhaps you could teach me some English. Mine is only so-so, but I would like to improve. Would you be able to help me?"

"Yes, of course. It would be my honor to help you learn English."

"Excellent. Could we start tomorrow evening around the same time?"

"Yes."

"Very good. I'll see you tomorrow then."

"Okay."

"And I suppose you remember the way out?"

"Yes, of course. Goodbye sir."

That was it. I strained to imagine what was really going on. Hoa had informed me about many things that went on at these get-togethers, but English was never one of them. He wanted help with English. Then I started wondering why he only wanted help with English. Did he not find me attractive? Did I do something wrong? Would Co Thu be furious with me tomorrow? Would I be in danger because I did not meet expectations? My mind twirled and turned as I left the room, descended the staircase and went out the front door. The tall, thin man had already pulled my motorbike around front and was waiting for me as I exited the building.

"Good evening, My Phuong. We will see you tomorrow."

How did he already know that? I pondered.

I nodded kindly at the man, got on the motorbike and rode off wondering what Hoa was doing and what was really going on. When I got home, I got something cold to drink and sat back in bed, waiting for Hoa and replaying the evening into my mind. I hadn't expected to be home at 9:35.

I dozed off around midnight and finally heard Hoa enter the room around 4AM. I immediately jumped out of bed, and she told me all about the intimate evening she spent with some official. Then she asked what had happened with me. When I told her that I met with Mr. Duc for five minutes so he could ask me if I could teach him English, she refused to believe me. We drank and laughed at each other for the next two hours until we both finally fell asleep.

The next evening, I arrived back at the guest house at nine PM, went to the large suite on the second floor, and talked to Mr. Duc in English for an hour. Then he sent me home. The same thing happened again on Monday and then Wednesday. Hoa couldn't believe that I was merely giving him English lessons. In fact, she started using *English lessons* as a rather unique euphemism. When we would be walking together past a Karaoke shop, she would say '*I wonder if they are giving English lessons tonight?*' or '*I had the best English lesson last night.*' I told her she could joke all she wanted but English was the only thing going on with Mr. Duc.

At work, Co Thu treated me strangely. She kept complimenting me on things like '*Oh, My Phuong, you gave that man an excellent cut today. Keep up the great work.'* It was like I could do no wrong.

Every second day or so, I would receive a phone call on my cell phone informing me of a lesson that evening, and so I would dress up in my best clothes and promptly show up to greet the city's top official. Mr. Duc puzzled me. He showed me great kindness and respect. When we studied English, he never sat directly beside me but always on the loveseat opposite the sofa. He seemed genuinely interested in practicing his English, and I admired him for that. He was, as far as I knew, the only politician in the country that I did admire. He was the only man I had been alone with that did not make an advance on me. He never once indicated that he wanted me for anything other than English lessons. I knew that this was not true, but I relished the fact that he was restrained to the extreme.

On the second Saturday evening of our English lessons, I met him for the sixth time in nine days. I had been wearing two different *ao dais* that I kept alternating every time I saw him. That night, however, I wore a short, tight-fitting black dress. I think I wanted to get his attention. In some bizarre way, I wanted to know if he really intended our meetings for something else all along. As he sat down in his normal location, I once again sat opposite him on the sofa.

"Mr. Duc. I wonder if it might be helpful if I sit closer to you. Maybe we could read this book together, and I could help you with your pronunciation."

I couldn't believe how forward I was being. It felt like a game, and I had to admit I was starting to enjoy it.

"If you think that would be best."

I got up out of my seat and went over and sat beside

him. My thigh rubbed up against his leg as I sat down. I knew this was the end of the line. I could have been content to be Mr. Duc's English teacher. I could have been content to sit opposite him, but it was eating me up. I'm sure he knew what it was doing to me. He treated me with respect, but I felt like his play-thing. I didn't know how to have a relationship built on respect. I only knew how to have one kind of relationship, and I could not tolerate him manipulating me like this anymore. For wasn't he manipulating me? Wasn't he just waiting to move in for the kill? It was easier to just give in and get on with it.

"Mr. Duc. Maybe we do not have to do so much talking this evening."

I reached out and felt his newly shaven face. Then I kissed him, and I became his.

I continued seeing Mr. Duc for "English lessons" three or four times a week over the next month. The tall skinny man always greeted me out front; Co Thu continued treating me with smiles and special compliments. Eventually I told Hoa that she was right about the English lessons. Over the course of that first month, I had grown quite fond of Mr. Duc. He treated me with kindness and dignity. He was gentle and soft-spoken; I always felt safe with him. He never warned me about keeping our secrecy or threatened me in anyway. I felt myself becoming loyal to him. It took me those four weeks to realize that I hadn't reaped any financial benefits from my relationship with Mr. Duc. He never once offered me money, but I really didn't care.

"Mr. Duc," I asked one evening. "Why did you ask me to come give you English lessons?"

"Why do you ask?"

"Did you have intentions for more than just English?"

"What do you think?"

"I think you did. I'm just not sure why you reacted the way you did."

"Well, in some ways you are right," he said. "I have never been too aggressive in relationships. They either work out or they do not. Love either happens or it does not. It cannot be forced. Do you not agree?"

I contemplated my response. I only knew about two kinds of love between a man and a woman: the first being forced upon me and the second being when I forced myself onto someone else in order to get something in return. Mutual love never just happened in my life.

"When I met my wife, I was a faculty member at Thai Nguyen University. She was a young teacher just out of university. She attracted me right away – not just her looks – but also her intellect and her compassion for others. I think she liked me for my level-headedness and my rather easy going manner. I suppose I wasn't too bad looking back then as well. And love just happened. I've been happily married to her for twenty years."

I turned my head away slightly as he said this. I wondered how someone could be happily married yet carry on an affair.

"Then why do you come here with me?" I asked boldly.

"There is *com* and then there is *pho*. I'm sure you understand."

I understood clearly. It was difference between a bowl of steamed rice and a bowl of noodle soup. The staple of every Vietnamese meal is *com* – steamed rice. *Com* is the bedrock – the foundation. Every family must have *com*. It is the substance you depend on for nourishment and sustenance. *Pho* is the Vietnamese beef noodle soup. You eat it at different times – perhaps late at night on the street, or early in the morning on the way to work. It is a quick tasty meal with exotic spices and a hint of chili. It's the anti-*com*. *Pho* is the treat that you give yourself when the everyday rice has become a little bland, predictable or unimaginative. His wife was the *com*. I was Mr. Duc's *pho*.

"But you know, you just don't eat *pho* from any place," he continued in his metaphor. "Some bowls may look attractive but taste salty, or bitter. Some *pho* places are not hygienic at all. *Pho* must be carefully selected and discretely enjoyed. But just because I enjoy *pho*, does not mean that *com* is not important to me. On the contrary, one could never live without rice, but one could conceivably live without *pho*."

I understood the meaning all too well.

"So I must make myself not seem too bitter," I said playfully.

"It is highly unlikely that you could ever be bitter. Besides, I like teachers, and you are helping me a lot with my English."

Mr. Duc smiled, stood up and went over to a large wooden cabinet that stood behind the wooden desk.

"I want to show you something. Come here."

I walked over to him as he opened the wardrobe doors revealing a large safe built into the wood. The safe door had two key holes like that of a safety deposit box. One key was already in one of the locks. Mr. Duc reached into his pocket and took out his key chain which had another one of the keys. He inserted it, turned the lock handle and the door creaked open.

"Do you like this?"

He held up a white gold necklace with eight diamond pendants hanging off it.

"It's beautiful."

"Like you. Here."

He reached over and put it around my neck. And then he kissed me.

"You shall wear this when you come. It is stunning on you. And you should also get a new wardrobe to match this necklace. Which reminds me. I haven't given you your monthly salary for teaching me yet."

He reached back into the safe and pulled out a stack of American bills and handed them to me. I shied away from taking them and tried to give them back, but he insisted. At that moment, I realized the trap I had been lured into from which there was no escape. It all seemed too obvious now. The money was part of it. It was way more than teaching money or even Karaoke bar hostess money. This was a sum of money that came with deep obligation and serious expectations. But it was more than just the money that frightened me. The open safe said it all. He not only showed me the location of the safe, he showed me freely how the safe could be opened. He showed me the contents of the safe. This was an open relationship – one that could not be made null or void. There was no walking away from this point on. I belonged to Mr. Duc, and there was nothing I could do to stop it. At that moment, those eight diamonds hung around my neck like eight millstones. I was drowning.

A Most Dangerous Customer

Playing the part of a prominent politician's mistress twisted my being every which way. Certain days I liked it. I liked dressing up and spending time with Mr. Duc. He treated me well, and I got more comfortable with him as time went on. I suppose in many ways I was becoming his second wife. Polygamy had a long history in Vietnam. My great uncle had three wives and seventeen children even though the practice is no longer legal. I was the dutiful second – showing up when needed – keeping my mouth quiet when not. The guest house became a second home to me. Cuong, the tall skinny man who always greeted me, went out of his way to make me comfortable. I continued cutting hair as normal, and Co Thu became very lenient with my hours. Everyone was showing me great favors. Hoa even became a little jealous of the kind of money I was bringing in – and it was significant. Mr. Duc gave me over $1000 USD a month for my English lessons. But at the same time, I was never so scared in my life. I saw no way out – no future – no lasting happiness. I would never be anything more than a mistress to Mr. Duc. What if he would tire of me? What if I did something to embarrass him? No one had ever threatened me to stay quiet about our relationship, and perhaps it was precisely this silence that scared me the most.

One Monday morning, Co Thu didn't show up to work. I stood outside the shop for fifteen minutes waiting for it to be opened. Co Ha, Thu's sister-in-law, finally showed up, and told me that Thu wouldn't be in, but that I was to go ahead and run the shop on my own until Hoa was scheduled to show up around ten. Around 9:30, my first customer pulled up in a black Nissan. Out of the car stepped a very stylishly dressed young woman approximately my own age. She was rather tall for a Vietnamese woman with long black hair and serious looking eyes.

"I'd like a head massage, all right?"

"Okay. You can sit over there. I'll get some warm water."

"Do you have a more private place?"

"Sure. You can enter the first room on the left."

She nodded and went down the hall and into the room where I first met Mr. Duc. I realized the rarity of the situation – not many women come to get only a head massage in a private room. As I entered the room, she sat glibly on the salon chair with legs crossed.

"What's your name?" she asked abruptly.

"My Phuong."

"My Phuong, how long have you worked here."

"Almost one year."

"I can tell by your accent that you aren't from around here. Where are you from?"

"Central highlands."

"Where exactly?"

"It's not important."

I didn't want to remember where I came from, and I wouldn't let her press me into it.

"So, a facial massage."

"Yes."

I got a cloth with warm water and started gently massaging her face.   At least she couldn't talk when I was doing this. After I rubbed with the cloth for ten minutes, I used my hands to rub her temples and then started massaging her head with my fingernails.

"Are you the only one here today?"

"So far. My boss couldn't make it today. Others will be in shortly."

"Is your boss Co Thu?"

"Yes. Do you know her?"

"I've heard about her from time to time. It seems that she is involved in several different business endeavors, is she not?"

"I'm afraid I don't know what you mean."

"Oh, I hear things. I'm sure you know what goes on around town."

"I'm sure I have no idea what you are talking about."

"That's too bad then. I was hoping that you would be able to help me."

"What do you need help with?"

I stopped massaging her head, and she sat up and looked right at me.

"I heard that there are some interesting parties and get-togethers sometimes. I'm always looking for a good time. I thought maybe you could help."

"What is your name," I asked her, keeping myself

rather skeptical of her intentions.

"Hue. Nguyen thi Thanh Hue. I'm sorry if you are suspicious of me. Someone told me that I could come to this shop and talk to My Phuong about certain issues."

"Who told you this?"

"Cuong."

"Which Cuong?"

"Cuong, one of the aids to councilman Duc. Do you know him? He is rather thin and tall and has a little wiry mustache."

"Yes, I know him," I nodded.

"Well, are you going to help me get some action around here or not?"

"Ah," I hesitated. This was nothing that I should be talking about, and I couldn't decide if the big black Nissan out front should be assurance that everything was all right or that there was something wrong. A girl trying to get into certain societies usually doesn't come from money. But at the same time, a person like that does bring some credibility to their story. Why else would they be snooping around?

"What's the matter?" she asked.

"Nothing. Let me ask my friend when she comes in. She might be able to help. How can I get in touch with you?"

"I can come back tomorrow."

"No, you shouldn't come here. You can stop by my place tomorrow evening. I rent a room at the large red house directly behind the district communal house. Do you know where that is?"

"Do you mean the house of Teacher Minh?"

"Yes, I do."

"I know exactly where that is at. He was my former teacher when I was a student at Hanoi University."

"Oh, that's great."

"You know when I lived in Hanoi, there were all kinds of interesting parties and events going on. I did some crazy stuff and met some people that, well, they'd probably kill me if I told anyone," she laughed and picked up her purse off the counter. "Actually, do you know what someone told me? I heard that our local councilman Mr. Duc keeps a beautiful young mistress, and he pays her a handsome sum each month just to, well, you know."

I faked a smile and went to the counter to clean up the water basin and towel.

"Do you know who it is?" she asked as she gently put her hand on my arm.

I shook my head and kept busy.

"Really, I'm sure you hear lots of juicy news in here."

I couldn't look her in the eye, and I tried to ignore the question.

"Come on," she kept pushing. "Do you know?"

I shook my head again.

"You do know, don't you?"

"I have to get out front and see if I have other customers," I said as I headed to the door.

"It's you, isn't it?"

I stopped dead in my tracks. I didn't know if I should acknowledge it or not.

"It's you."

I turned around and looked at her.

"Why is this so important to you?" I asked. I felt like I was glaring.

She looked me over up and down as if to see if I had

the appropriate body and face for a councilman's mistress.

"It's not so important. I could see why any man would choose you. You are very beautiful."

We stood in silence for a few moments as she kept looking at me in a very disturbing manner.

"My Phuong and Mr. Duc," she said somewhat under her breath.

"It's not good to spread rumors around. They can be dangerous," I said still not admitting the truth but certainly not denying it.

"I wouldn't dream of it. So, I'll see you tomorrow," she said and exited out the door before me. As she got in the black Nissan to drive off, Hoa entered in a hurry.

"What was she doing here?" Hoa said.

"Who?"

"That woman. That's Mr. Duc's daughter."

I suddenly felt dizzy and weak-kneed. I nearly fainted, and Hoa caught me and sat me down in one of the salon chairs.

"What was she doing here?"

"I've been tricked. She knows that I'm Duc's mistress."

"Oh my God! What are we going to do?"

"We have to talk to Co Thu. Why didn't she come in today?" I said with a sick feeling in my stomach, and I ran back to the bathroom and threw up. My head was spinning, and my heart pounding. What was I going to do? Hoa entered the bathroom, handed me a damp wash cloth and rubbed my back.

"We have to talk to Co Thu. When is she coming in," I said.

"She's not. She was arrested this morning."

"Arrested? For what?" I asked in shock.

"Societal corruption. My guess is that someone is getting squeezed from above, and someone else is going to take the fall for it. This is bad. Really bad."

"What are we going to do?"

"We need to be patient and wait this out. Maybe nothing will come of it."

We heard the door buzz as someone entered the shop.

"Come on. Now we have customers. We can sort this out later. Don't worry," said Hoa.

It was too late. I was already well beyond worry.

Visitors

Nothing out of the ordinary happened the rest of the day, but I felt nervous and sick to my stomach the whole time. I never received a text message from Mr. Duc to meet him that night, but that fact was not anything terribly out of the ordinary. I never saw him every night anyways, but for some reason I attached great importance to not receiving a message that day. I tried to think rationally about everything, but the more I thought about it, the more anxious I became. At around 8:30 PM, Thu's sister showed up again.

"I'm going to close the shop now," she said as she dangled a large ring of keys.

"How is Co Thu? Is everything okay?"

"Yes, no problem. She is feeling a little sick today. She'll be back to work tomorrow."

I glanced slyly over to Hoa, who shook her head very slowly telling me not to let on that I knew anything.

"Okay, so I'll see you at nine in the morning."

Co Thu's sister grunted a 'yes' and Hoa and I were off to try and get through the night and see what would happen tomorrow. We would most definitely be using the bottle opener on my keychain very liberally tonight.

Hoa and I both went into the shop around nine the next morning, but it was still closed. We waited. We waited until 9:30 and then 10 but no one ever came, so we finally went home. We wondered the meaning of this, but decided that we would just need to wait everything out. Hoa used her free day to visit her sister in Hanoi, so she caught the 11 AM bus while I headed back to my room and went back to bed. I was still feeling the effects of a restless sleep coupled with too much alcohol. I was gone to the world in about five minutes.

At about 12:30, I heard the outside gate swing open and the teacher's dogs started barking and yipping. The chickens scattered, but I paid little attention and turned over to go back to sleep. A moment later, I heard the door to my room open, and I turned my head slightly, barely opening my eyes to see who it was. There was a quick movement across my room to my bed. Someone grabbed my hair and yanked it back quickly. Pain shot through my head.

"You little whore."

I looked up and Hue, Mr. Duc's daughter stood over me pulling my head back with my hair.

I let out a scream.

"Shut up, whore," Hue yelled at me.

Another young woman was with her. She came and stood directly in front of me.

"This is what you get for seducing our father."

She took her nails and ripped them across my left cheek as Hue continued to hold me up by the hair. Blood started running down my face and they mixed with the tears and screams that I kept yelling.

"Go ahead and scream you bitch. But you are going to pay for what you did."

The second girl then ripped her nails across my neck and Hue let go of my hair and punched me in the eye. I fell back down into the bed, my legs and arms flailing as they forced themselves on top of me. That's when I glanced up and saw a third woman in the room – an older woman dressed very fashionably.

"Stop," she said as she came towards me. Both of the girls stopped fighting with me and stood off to the sides as she approached. I sat up in the bed trembling, a broken animal cowered in defeat, but I looked straight at her.

Suddenly the door to my room opened again, and in walked Teacher Minh looking concerned. He stopped cold when he saw the three women around me. Mrs. Duc looked back at him and motioned to the door with her head. He looked at me for a moment, and then he looked back at Mrs. Duc, nodded slightly and turned around and left. I would have no salvation from my fate. I was at the mercy of Duc's wife and daughters.

"So you are the skinny little whore who has been sleeping with my husband?" she asked and glared at me as I shook uncontrollably. "I will not be made a mockery of. You think you can use your pretty face and young figure to woo away a prestigious man like my husband? I know the likes of you. Money. Always looking for money. They say politicians are corrupt, but no, it's the low class whores like you who seduce with evil intent – you are the corruptors. You will get what is coming to you."

She held in her hand a bamboo stick.

"Turn her around."

The two daughters grabbed my arms and tried to twist me over onto my stomach. I resisted fiercely until Mrs. Duc smacked me across the face with the stick. I then relented and turned over. One of the girls grabbed my shirt and ripped it off revealing my bare back. Then Mrs. Duc started slashing my back with the bamboo time after time after time. I cringed with every lash. She kept hitting me perhaps three dozen times. I had lost track. I moaned in pain and cried in my pillow. Then one of the daughters, and it didn't really matter which one, took their nails and started ripping them firmly down my back. The pain was unbearable. I could do nothing but cry. After another five minutes, they turned me over. My back burnt with pain and blood dripped all over my bed. I cried and cried as I covered up my bare chest with a sheet.

"The girl looks sad," Mrs. Duc said smugly. "You should be sad, whore."

I looked down, afraid to glance at their smirking faces.

"Will you ever see my husband again?" she asked.

I kept looking straight down. Hue slapped me strongly across the face.

"Answer her. Will you ever see my father again?"

I shook my head.

"You aren't as stupid as you look. If you do, then this is what you can expect."

The second daughter punched me twice in my right eye.

I felt dizzy and wanted to pass out.

"Okay, whore, I believe you. But if you are foolish and try to see him again, I'll kill you."

Mrs. Duc glared at me with intense hatred. I didn't doubt her word. Then she held up the stick high once again and hit me with all her might across my face. I fell onto the bed and just closed my eyes in a state of semi-consciousness. Apparently they left at that point. I lay in bed for several hours before I finally came around and tried to pull myself together. My back throbbed in pain. I lightly put a thin cotton shirt around my body and went out to the spigot in the courtyard to clean up a little. I stood over the spigot for a moment and looked around the courtyard. I noticed Teacher Minh looking at me through the slits in the slotted glass windows of his living room. When he saw me looking back at him, he closed them quickly. I squatted down and wet a towel rubbing it slowly over my face. My back was too raw to touch and the thought of water on it pained me even more. It would have to remain as is for the moment. My thoughts zoned out for several minutes and I don't know how long I squatted there with the water running. I finally, got up went into my room, and ripped all of the blood stained sheets off the bed. Then I sat down and again wondered what I was supposed to do. It was at that moment I noticed all of the contents of my purse emptied onto the floor. I looked for my wallet, but it was gone. All my money was gone. I had nothing. I couldn't even escape Thai Nguyen if I wanted to. I sat back down and held a mirror in front of me, seeing for the first time my two black eyes which were swollen. I also had red puffy fingernail scars down both of my cheeks. I wanted to die. Co Thu couldn't help me, and Hoa was away. My instincts told me to run, but I had nowhere to go and very little money. I sat and pondered my slim prospects when Teacher Minh came to the door.

"My Phuong," he called in.

I tightened up my clothes around me and closed my eyes as pain pulsed through my back as the shirt came in contact with it.

"Yes."

He stepped two feet inside the door. The room was rather dimly lit, so it was doubtful that he saw the extent of my injuries.

"I want you out of here. Tonight."

"Teacher Minh. Please, I need you to help me. Please."

"You need to get out of here. Be out by eight."

"But Teacher, I have nowhere to go. I—"

"Out. I cannot be associated with these kinds of things. I need to have respectable tenants here."

He turned around and left. He and his family had always been kind to me. Over the past year, I had offered several times to cut his children's hair free of charge, and I always enjoyed talking in English to Teacher Minh. But this obviously was too much to handle. Mrs. Duc showing up at his house and raking over a girl was a powerful message. He had become too closely associated with messy business and wanted no part of it. I couldn't blame him, but his actions and words hurt me deeply. I had no one but myself, and at that point I doubted I would ever rise again. I just wanted to die.

At that moment, a text message beeped on my phone. I reached over and pressed *Read*.

"*Meet me tonight at 9. I want to see you. Duc.*"

The Last Meeting

I had nothing more to lose, and I held dearly to the belief that I had an ever so slim amount to gain by meeting Mr. Duc one more time. Perhaps he would show me some sympathy if he saw this pathetic, battered figure coming towards him. Perhaps I was more than just an evening fling to him. I clung to nothing else but this dim hope.

From the time Teacher Minh left my room, I had spent every moment in a painful daze. I slowly tried to collect my things, but I ached all over and I couldn't even remember what items belonged to me and what to Hoa. Around 7, I finally got up the courage to call Hoa. I told her everything, and she was in tears pleading with me not to go anywhere till she got back. I told her I wouldn't be there much longer. She yelled at me to not go to Duc's that night. She asked me to put Teacher Minh on the phone, but I couldn't bear to go and face him again, so I refused her. She was furious at me. Finally, I hung up on Hoa, unable to put up with her frantic talk anymore. My life precariously teetered on the brink – one last night – one last meeting. I realized that I could be dead by midnight, and it didn't seem like such an undesirable outcome.

I readied two small bags and left many other possessions behind. I had a small amount of money that had been stashed away, but it wouldn't do much for me. I piled the bags one of top of the other in the basket of my Honda motorbike. Without an electric starter, I would have had to walk because I never could have kick started the thing in my condition. I keep my head down and looked only straight ahead as I started the bike and left the courtyard. Spying eyes followed my every move. Everyone in my neighborhood would have known about me by now. Neighbors, once friendly, shielded their faces and looked away as I drove past, only then to turn back around and follow my trail out of sight with their eager eyes. I twice drove around the city, past the clock tower, down towards Mo Bach and the university, out past the bus station and then left down the main drag back to the clock tower downtown. I had nowhere to go. The only standing invitation I had was from the gates of hell itself – the place that got me into this predicament in the first place. I circled three or four times around the clock tower but with every turn the big hand approached twelve. The clock possessed me – I felt bound to obey its call. There was no other force in the world working for me at that moment except for that clock, prodding, cudgeling, and nudging me forward to my destiny. I couldn't pull away from its magic. A bus came barreling into the traffic circle. If I only had the courage to quickly turn sharply right into the path of the bus, it could all be over, but it passed without incident and I caught one last glimpse of the clock as I drove straight towards the market. It read 8:57. I turned past the market and went down a few blocks, past the movie theater and into the courtyard of the People's Council Guest House. The gate was open, but the courtyard was completely empty. No one stood at the door and the guard house too stood vacant – an oddity.

I dismounted my motorbike, grabbed my two bags – one in each hand for I could not imagine placing either of them over my back – and tepidly walked through the open front doors. The lights in the large entrance hall burnt brightly, but no one was in sight. It was the first time I ever came here without Cuong greeting me. Perhaps it was a warning sign, but I had long ago passed the safe route. Once you fall off a cliff, there are no more warning signs. Each time I lifted my foot to go up another step, pain shot through my body, but I continued the long trek to the second floor guest house room on the left – the one I knew so well. The large wooden double doors had six large panes of glass in each one. Curtains had been drawn from the inside, so I could not see in. I took a deep breath, and with much effort pushed down the stiff metal handle that unlatched the door with the sound of a click-click-click-click-click. I slowly opened it fully, picked up my second bag which I had placed on the ground and walked into the room closing the door behind me. The room was empty, but I noticed that the door to the balcony was open because the door's full length curtain flapped in the wind. I put down my bags and walked slowly towards the balcony sensing Duc's presence. Perhaps all would be well.

As I went to pull back the curtain, a hand from the balcony grabbed my wrist and twisted it back towards me.

"The little whore who won't learn her lesson," Duc's

daughter Hue said as she pushed me backwards towards the sitting area.

Once again, I was trapped. I only wanted to die. Hue pushed me into the couch, my back writhing in pain, as she approached and started slapping me across the cheeks — the cheeks that were already swollen and scarred from the afternoon. I had no fight left within me. She slapped me mercilessly while swearing and yelling at me at the top of her lungs. I noticed two other figures standing around her as well — Mrs. Duc and the other daughter. I gave into the pain and took each blow flopping my head back and forth like an inanimate baby doll being shaken by a little girl. When Hue stopped, the second daughter came up into my face and spit on me. Then Mrs. Duc approached carrying a pair of scissors. Their words and insults twirled around the room, but I barely noticed them anymore. I felt semi-unconscious partially unaware of what happened to me. But when I saw the scissors, I jumped backwards in a last attempt of a survival instinct. I wanted to die, but I still didn't want to be stabbed. As she came closer, I yelled out for the first time "No, No." She put the scissors up toward my neck. I ducked and closed my eyes — and then she cut off my long flowing hair on which people often complimented me. She threw the pair of scissors on the couch and leaned over to my ear.

"Your lover is coming. Now he will see how beautiful you really are."

Mrs. Duc glanced over to the other side of the suite. There stood Mr. Duc, who had entered from one of the side rooms on the far end. Mrs. Duc, with her two daughters by her side, looked over at her husband and nodded slightly. Then she smiled at him quickly turning back at me. Her glib grin declared victory. I, the defeated, the bruised, the weary, the hopeless, sat on the brink of death. I wanted it more than anything else. Perhaps he would do it. Perhaps her grim grin was my death warrant. Perhaps she would make him do her bidding. Or maybe that's when the wiry Cuong would make his appearance – to finish the job. One thing seemed certain; I would no longer be a problem for this family after tonight.

"Farewell," she said to me calmly and walked out of the room with her daughters behind her.

Several minutes passed and I seemed to almost black out – sitting dazed waiting for the crushing final blow. Then I finally noticed Mr. Duc standing over top of me. Arms folded, staring right at me.

"You should have known better than to open your mouth."

I kept my eyes looking straight down.

"You could have been something more than just a mistress. You had it all, but look at you now. This will be how I'll remember you. Ugly and swollen."

He didn't flinch from his posturing – arms folded, head tilted to the left. He had a smug grin on his face. He seemed to be a completely different person.

"They really did you good. Turned a masterpiece into a worthless piece of trash."

His words hurt every wound of my body. I marveled at how someone so dignified, so refined and in control could turn into a predator – licking the wounds of the one he tortured. Gleefully singing death's serenade.

"It was all your fault," he continued. "From the day I entered your shop for a shave, you had your eyes on me. You seduced me. You got into my head with your pretty face and young body. But I see your tricks. Yes, I see your tricks."

He leaned into me.

"And you got what you deserved."

I raised my arm as if to hit him, but he caught my wrist. Tears ran down my face, they made my wounds burn. I hated him. He rubbed his hand along my chin.

"Such a pity. You used to be so beautiful."

He got up and went over to the desk and lit a cigarette.

"What's to become of me?" I feebly asked through the tears.

"Ha," he laughed. "What's to become of you? It will be hard to keep your naughty deeds under wraps."

"Are you going to kill me?"

"Don't be silly. But I want something to be very clear."

He quickly came to the sofa and grabbed me around the neck pushing me backwards. The pain shot through my body, especially from the wounds on my back.

"You will leave Thai Nguyen and never come back. You will never speak of this to anyone, or you will be dead."

"Stop. It hurts me," I pleaded.

He continued the pressure around me.

"Do you understand?" he aggressively increased the pressure around my neck. I was choking. I couldn't breathe. "Do you understand?"

I couldn't have nodded in affirmation if I wanted to. The pain surrounded me. I gagged for breath, but there was none. And in my last attempt at life, I reached around with my right hand for anything at all for which to defend myself. I found my purse and felt for my key chain as he continued yelling at me. I felt a hard plastic card in my hand. With all of my remaining strength, I thrust the card right into Mr. Duc's eye. He recoiled back, immediately to cover his eye with his hands.

"Ahhhhh!" he yelled in pain.

Blood began squirting down his face as he continued screaming and yelling. I got up immediately and went toward the desk, trying to get behind it for at least some protection. He came after me immediately, grabbed me around the waist and threw me against the desk. I desperately searched for another weapon. I finally kneed him in the stomach and he fell backward just enough for me to get out of his grip. He still held his eye and blood continued to gush down his face. He ranted and raved at me as I skirted behind the desk.

"Come here you witch. I will end this right now."

"Stay away from me," I said with deepening conviction. "You are the one that caused all of this. You are to blame, not me."

"You've assaulted a party official. You will go to jail for this, if you survive this night. Come here now."

"Go to hell. You are just like every other corrupt official. Like the ones that killed my parents."

"Come here now!"

He lunged around the corner of the table at me. He took his hand away from his eye, and it looked like part of his eyeball was hanging out. I panicked and picked up the small *phuc, loc, tho* three figured statue made of marble. I held the heavy symbol of happiness, luck, and longevity with both hands over my head and hurled it at him with all my might as he was no further than four feet away from me. The ridged edge of the statue cut into his forehead and stopped him from advancing. He staggered for a moment, trying to catch his balance on the edge of the desk, but then he collapsed, hitting his head violently on the side of the desk and sprawling out on the floor. I backed up a couple of feet and just stared at him for a moment. The sudden silence was eerie. I wondered if he was dead, but I did not have the nerve to go near him.

Run, I thought. *Leave.*

I ran to the sofa and grabbed my keys, and then I went to the door and picked up my bags when I stopped suddenly. I thought of the key in his pocket. What did I have to lose? I could think of nothing. I put down my bags and ran quickly over to his body which still wasn't moving. He lay on his stomach with his face away from me. I cautiously kneeled down beside him and slowly reached my hand into his front pocket. I had to nudge his body up a little bit to reach down to the bottom and find his key ring. I retrieved it quickly, then jumped back two steps jittery and afraid he might stir. My heart pounded; adrenaline ripped through my throbbing body, but my mind was clear. I went to the large wooden cabinet from which he extracted my monthly salary for "English lessons", and opened the door. The safe stood before me with one key in one of the key holes and the other just waiting for its mate. I put the key in and turned it. Then I pushed down on the safe handle and the door creaked open wide. In the back corner sat a large stack of cash. I ran to the suite door, grabbed my backpack and emptied all my clothes onto the floor. I ran back to the safe and stuffed stack after stack of US 50s and 100s into the bag. I stuffed and shoved and nudged in the blood money. Then

I saw my diamond necklace, the one Mr. Duc made me wear every time. I put it into my pants pocket and then rushed past his body once more. He remained still and unresponsive. I picked up my other bag and ran out into the hallway and down the stairs. The place remained completely vacant — no doubt the Duc family planned it that way so they could discreetly take care of their little problem. I ran on adrenaline out the main hall door and to my motorbike parked off to the right.

"Come on, come on," I stumbled with my keys trying to get it into the ignition. I did. It turned. I started it. I zoomed out of the courtyard and into the street.

"I have to get out of Thai Nguyen. I have to leave. No, I have to leave the country."

My mind went back and forth replaying everything over and over. I didn't notice my pain at all.

"Hung, maybe Hung can help me."

After about ten minutes, I ended up on the backside of the university where Hung rented a room. I sat idling on top of the dike road overlooking the university. The road was pitch-black at night with no streetlights. I called Hung.

"Hello."

"Hung. It's me. I need to see you now."

"I'm about ready to go out, I—"

"Hung. Now. Up on Mo Bach road. Hurry. I need you now."

"OK, I'll be there in a minute."

Two minutes later, the headlights from Hung's bike lit up my face as he came to a stop.

"What in the world happened to you?"

"Nothing. I'm in trouble. Lots of trouble."

"What happened?"

"I can't tell you. I just can't tell you. But it's bad, real bad. I need your help."

"What's going on?"

"No, trust me. It's much better if you don't know anything. I'm sure tomorrow they will come asking questions."

"Who?"

"The police. Hung, just listen. Did you say you had a contact that can move people?"

"Yeah, but, I don't know. It's dangerous."

"I need to get out of the country. Now."

"My Phuong, I don't know. You can't just leave the country. You don't have that kind of money. I mean, these are serious individuals."

"Money is not a problem."

"What do you mean 'money is not problem'? What in the world is going on?"

"Hung, I'll pay you $1000 right now to get me in contact with these people."

"A thousand dollars? Are you serious?"

"Look at me Hung. Do I not look desperate?"

"Yes, you do. Let me make a call."

He parked the bike and walked away about fifteen feet and started an animated conversation in which I had to strain to understand only every few words. He finally put the phone down, holding the receiver over his pants to block the sound.

"Ten thousand dollars," he said to me.

I nodded. He looked at me, surprised, and then walked away to finish his conversation. After a minute, he approached me again.

"You are in luck, if you really have that kind of cash. There is a freighter leaving Haiphong tonight at 4AM. There will be several stowaways on it. You sure you want to get into this?"

"Where is it going?"

"America."

"Yes. I have no other choice."

"Okay, it's 9:45. The last bus to Haiphong leaves in fifteen minutes. You need to get moving now."

"Okay," I said appreciatively.

"Here's what you need to do. At exactly 3AM, be at 12 Tran Hung Dao Street.   You will meet a man called "August Revolution" and he'll do the rest. You need to pay him up front."

"Okay. I'll do it."

"My Phuong, what is going on?"

"You'll know by tomorrow. But just remember one thing; things did not happen the way that the papers will report it tomorrow. Remember that, okay?"

"Okay," said Hung looking perplexed.

I reached into my backpack and pulled out a wad of 50s.

"Here, this is well more than $1000. For all your trouble."

He looked shocked and took the money without question.

"I think it is better that I don't know. You poor girl, look at you. And your hair."

"It's okay. Can I have your cap?"

He handed it to me.

"I think you paid enough for it," he smiled.

I put the cap down over my head.

"And this bag, I can't take it. I need to go lighter."

"Well, from what it sounds like, I don't think I should have your belongings in my possession."

"Yes, of course," I said realizing how foolish that was. "Goodbye Hung."

"Goodbye My Phuong."

"12 Tran Hung Dao Street, right?"

"Yes," he said.

I started the bike and took off down the road. Just past the university stood several large dumpsters. I pulled over and reached into my duffel bag pulling out about four pieces of clothing. Then I threw the duffel into the trash bin and tore up the street with only my purse, my backpack of money and these few items of clothing.   The bus station was only three minutes up the road. I stopped the bike on the street outside the gate, threw the keychain into my purse and then ran through the main gate to the ticket counter. I kept my cap down over my eyes as much as possible.

"One ticket to Haiphong."

"It's pulling out right now."

"Okay."

I handed her the money and she gave me the paper ticket. I ran to the bus and entered. Luckily, it was only half full. We pulled out of the gate, and I felt some relief. As we went through the first traffic circle, sirens could be heard behind us. Three police cars, roaring as loudly as possible, raced up from behind. My heart pounded as surely they came for me. But they raced past us, turned left, and headed downtown towards the clock tower, the market, the cinema, and the People's Council Guest House. Our bus quietly went straight and within minutes had exited Thai Nguyen City. I was on my way.

I leaned my head against the window and cried.

"Dear God. Dear God," I said under my breath.

I hadn't prayed in a long time. I was raised a Protestant, but I left all that in the south after my parents died.

"Dear God. I'm so afraid. I'm so afraid."

There was nothing else to pray. I sobbed quietly as the bus darted through the night, beeping its horn, swerving left and right around motorbikes, cars, and the occasional animal. After some thirty minutes, my tears gave way to sleep.

About an hour into the trip, the bus screeched to a full stop which jerked my torn-up face into the seat in front of me. Three water buffalo stood directly in the middle of the road. The bus beeped its horn incessantly until they slowly plodded out into the darkness. My face throbbed, and I reached into my purse to find some Panadol, swallowing four of them whole. I then caught a glance of my cell phone and thought that perhaps they could trace my location if I used it. I pried open the back of it, removed the SIM card and threw it out the open window. Then I pulled out my compact which had a mirror and battery powered light, daring to look at my face – a face I barely recognized. I reached to pull my key chain out of my purse. I knew I wouldn't need those anymore. As I glanced down, I saw Martin Kinney's license had some strange shading over it. I shined the light on Martin's face and there were blood splatters all around. I then realized that Martin's license was the hard plastic card that I plunged into Mr. Duc's eye.

I took it off the key ring, and placed it into my wallet.

"Thank you Martin. You really are a good luck charm. I hope you have some more magic in you. I need it."

We arrived in Haiphong about 1:45. I had an hour to find Tran Hung Dao Street and to try and organize the large stash of cash in my backpack. I had never been in Haiphong before, so I didn't know where to start. However, Tran Hung Dao was a very prominent general in Vietnamese history who thrice repelled Chinese invasions. It was such a common and popular street name in every city that it usually was in a very central location. I would walk down the main streets and hope to find it. I found an open public restroom off the back end of a large market complex beside the bus station. It reeked of urine and only a small incandescent light dimly lit the room. I went into a stall which had a normal squat pot. There was very little room, but I decided to use this place to reorganize my money. I must have had more than $100,000 with varying stacks of 100s, 50s, and 20s. I put one stack of 100s in my underwear and a stack of 50s in my bra. I put several stacks of cash in my purse and a couple more wrapped in the extra clothes I brought. The rest I left in the backpack. I understood what my odds were with the type of characters I would meet that night. I had to give myself the best chance to get away, and by dispersing the money into several locations, I hoped I would be able to keep something. I took a deep breath, opened the stall door, and walked out of the bathroom.

I walked through the center of the large park by the bus station and ended up at a small square which had a French-era theater on one end. This looked to be the city center. I noticed a main drag lined with various shops which headed slightly downhill opposite the theater. This looked to be the old section of town and an excellent place to find Tran Hung Dao Street, and down three blocks on the right I found the street sign. I was relieved. I walked down the street a short way and squatted in the shadows of a small alley. I didn't want to be early. I felt exhausted, but I had to make sure I didn't fall asleep. Thirty minutes passed as I squatted in a trance-like state. No one had come by or bothered me. I felt fortunate.

At 2:55, I walked down about one block and stood outside the gate at number twelve. The house was dark. I was afraid to ring the bell. I jiggled the handle on the gate, and suddenly two large German Shepherds charged the gate and barked ferociously. After a few seconds a voice yelled out through the window.

"Quiet. Quiet."

The dogs quieted immediately and out walked a middle aged man wearing no shirt and only boxer shorts. He came right up to the gate and shined a flashlight on me. He looked at my wounds and scars and nodded.

"What do you want?"

"Hung sent me."

"Who do you want?"

"August Revolution."

He paused for a moment and looked back at me. I held the $10,000 in my right hand behind my back.

"Money."

I handed it to him. He immediately went into the house. I took out a stack of 50s fully expecting having to pay more. I waited at the gate for several minutes, then a young man in his late twenties came out. He unlocked the gate and grabbed me by the neck.

"Listen. There is too much going on tonight. Just get

out of here. We can't help you."

"I can pay more."

"What do you got?"

I handed him the other stack of 50s. He looked at me in a peculiar manner. Perhaps it was usually not so easy to extract extra money.

"What's in the bag?"

"Just my belongings."

"Where did you get all this money?"

I didn't answer. He gently rubbed his hands over the wounds on my face, and eventually shook his head.

"Let's go," he said.

I got on the back of his motorbike. I realized what I was doing was a longshot. I had just given a complete stranger – one involved in criminal activity – $15,000 to get me out of the country. For all I knew, he could have been taking me to the outskirts of town to kill me in the quiet of the night. I didn't trust him at all, but I had no other available options.

After about ten minutes, we pulled up within sight of the shipyard. Large container vessels stood straight up out of the river, and I wondered if one of them would be my salvation. The driver pulled off the side of the road.

"Wait here."

He walked about fifty feet away from me, made a quick phone call, and finally came back to me.

"Down that way about thirty meters, there is a light post. When you get to the light post, walk to the fence. There is a portion of the fence which is loose. Pull it up and crawl under it. There will be a trash dumpster to your left. Wait behind it."

I nodded.

"Go now," he said forcefully.

I grabbed my backpack and walked down until I got to the light post. I walked to the fence and found that part of it was curled up at the bottom. I pulled it up slightly and noticed that it was big enough to get through. I laid down flat on my stomach, pulled up the fence with my right hand and slowly wedged myself under it. When I was halfway through, my right hand couldn't hold it anymore and the metal wire came down directly on the wounds of my back. Pain shot through my whole body, but I kept shimmying until I was finally clear of the fence. The dumpster stood off to the left just as he said, and I quickly ran and huddled down behind it. I marveled at all that happened in my life to bring me to this point. If my mother were still alive, she would be ashamed of me. I knew that for a fact. A karaoke hostess, a thief, and a murderer. Is any mother ever prepared to hear those words to describe her daughter? *It wasn't my fault*, I thought. *What choice did I have? This was the lot that God gave me.* My body ached; my head hurt; my heart was empty. I was ready for the end for many hours now, but I kept moving forward; I kept hoping; I kept going on without really understanding why.

"Dear God. Dear God," I kept praying.

There was nothing else to say.

After about twenty minutes, two dark figures came around the corner of the dumpster. They stood looking at me for a moment.

"What do you have for us," one of them finally said.

I had another stack of cash in my hand. I had just randomly grabbed it out of the backpack.

"Here," I offered it to him.

"Let me see your bag," said the other one and grabbed the backpack from my grip. He opened it up to see ten or so stacks of bills in various denominations.

"Look here," he said to his buddy.

They both gawked over the large amount of cash in their possession.

"This will do. Come quickly."

We walked down through several rows of containers. The engine of a large container ship roared right in front of us. We walked onto the ship through some sort of gangplank and were quickly met by a merchant marine who started complaining about me. The men opened the bag and showed him the stash, and then he directed me down a small alleyway and out a door which led to a massive stack of containers in front of us. We walked down between the stacks until we came to a certain blue container with the words "Essex Four" on the outside. He unlatched the back and opened the door. There were a large stack of wooden crates that towered almost to the ceiling.

"Climb up to the top and then over to the back of the container. There is a room there where you will stay during your trip."

This seemed absurd. A room at the back of the container? I had to climb crates in my condition? I nodded and started the climb. The crates were staggered enough that I could get up to the top without any difficulty. There was about a four foot dark tunnel in the center of the container. This must have been the route, because there was no other way to go. I crawled on the tops of the crates through the darkness, thinking that I would probably die in the deep recesses of the Essex Four container. After I crawled a ways, I saw a dim light ahead which gave me tremendous hope. I inched toward the light, keeping my head down, focusing on the faint hopeful sight which became brighter and brighter. As I got closer, there was a buzzing sound of some engine roaring. I finally came upon a rather large wooden structure with a hole in the center. I peered into the hole and saw two other people inside.

"Hello," I said from the top. "Is there any way down?"

"You have to jump," said one of the two females there.

I turned my body around so my legs extended down into the wooden room. It was about three meters down, so I balanced my arms on the edges of the opening and jumped down. My feet hit the floor hard and gave way as I crashed painfully to the floor. I lay on the wood floor and swore under my breath as the pain throbbed through my body. The room was about three meters square. A single light bulb illuminated the makeshift wooden room and a small fan blew from one of the corners. The constant drone of an engine pulsated throughout the room.

"What's that noise?" I asked.

"That's a generator blowing oxygen into the room," said one of my roommates. She was a middle aged woman with a large scar down her left cheek.

"What's your name?"

"I'm My Phuong," I said feeling like I was in some bizarre dimension of time and place. My senses completely confused my head as I wondered if I, perhaps, was dreaming all of this.

"I'm Hang."

"I'm Huong. You are messed up."

"Do we have to stay in here the whole time?" I asked.

Huong came over to me and looked me over real carefully.

"What happened to you?"

"I fell down some stairs."

"Yeah, sure. Those were some nasty stairs. We have to stay in here during the day. At night, someone will come and let us out for a few hours."

"But why does it have to be so secretive?"

"There's about twenty crew members on board this freighter, but only four know about us. They need to keep it that way, so we are locked in here," said Hang. "But we can't leave here tonight. The first twenty-four hours, they said we would have to stay put. That will get us far enough out to sea."

"What if I have to pee or ..."

"There's a jug here. Welcome to our voyage to hell."

"No," I said. "I've just come from hell."

Freedom

It was after 4 AM that we started moving. The first hour and a half was very smooth, but it quickly became obvious when the ship passed from the inland shipping lanes and hit the open sea. All three of us started holding our stomachs and swaying our heads back and forth. I threw up first into a plastic bag and Hang and Huong followed my lead shortly thereafter. The insufferable stench from the three bags of vomit gradually started seeping out, but we could do nothing but suffer through it.

"How long will we have to live like this?"

"About two weeks," replied Huong.

I sat in the corner, leaning my left arm against the wooden wall and trying to keep my back comfortable, but it was nearly impossible. I mercifully fell asleep shortly after that and was gone for twelve hours, though I intermittently faded in and out, searching for a comfortable position and swaying with the motion of the ship. I had no food, and Huong and Hang were reluctant to share theirs. They told me that I would get one meal a day during the middle of the night once the first twenty-four hour period expired. So I anguished in pain and hunger, also trying not to think about having to relieve myself. Hours dragged on slowly. Huong talked non-stop about her desire to get a good job and meet up with her brother in Vancouver at some point. Hang and I said very little. I watched our only source of light the small bulb dangle up and down. The low humming of the generator tucked in the front of the container became nothing but white noise after several hours. My ears couldn't really focus on the noises around me with all the repugnant smells and piercing pain pre-occupying me.

I started looking for trivial things to do to keep me occupied. I organized my purse, kept looking at my beaten face in my compact, and filed my nails. At one point, Martin Kinney's license caught my eye at the bottom of my purse. I reached down and lifted it out into the light. I looked at Martin's face. I found it ironic that his face looked beat up as well with Mr. Duc's blood splotches on it. I took out a cloth, dabbed a little bit of drinking water on it and began to wipe it clean. I stared at Martin's funny face. It was round and red with that scraggly red beard. But unlike most other mug shots, he had a beautiful smile – *jolly* would be the word. His eyes looked kind. I kept looking at him and the thought hit me that he actually looked like a baby. A baby with a half grown beard. I couldn't contain myself and let out a small chuckle. It was the first time I smiled in many, many hours. Hang noticed my amusement.

"What's that?"

"Nothing."

"No really. What is it?"

"It's something that saved my life."

"Let me see it."

"No."

"Let me see it," she stood up and walked over two feet and ripped it out of my hand. "It's just some foreigner's driver's license."

She looked skeptically at me and then tossed it against the wall. I picked it up and put it back in my purse. No one would ever touch my good luck charm again. I put my head back against the wall, and eventually nodded off again.

A banging from the top woke me suddenly around hour twenty-four. I looked to see a Vietnamese man attach a hanging ladder down into our room.

"Come on. You can come out for a little bit now."

We didn't hesitate. We took the bags full of vomit and a container of urine and climbed to the top of the wooden room. Then we crawled along the wooden crates and down and out the back of the container. The chill in the air felt invigorating, and the freshness immediately lifted my spirits. Another Vietnamese man was standing outside our container.

"Walk down there between this row of containers. You can spend a little time at the front of the ship."

I walked through the canyon wall of containers and then out to the small opening on the very front of the ship. Stars were out in full force. They had a couple small bowls of rice and soup which I greeted with reckless abandon. I felt so hungry that this simple meal tasted more like one of Mr. Duc's feasts he often had for me. *Maybe I could do this,* I thought. Perhaps. After I ate, they showed me to a restroom where I could freshen up, and then I returned to the front of the ship and just gazed into the blackness.

After another hour, one of the sailors came to warn us that we had to get back in the container in about ten minutes. I nodded, and then thought of something.

"Do you have a shortwave radio?" I asked.

"Sure."

"Can you get the Vietnamese news broadcasts?"

"Yes, we get the *Dai Tieng Noi Viet Nam*."

The Voice of Vietnam. Would it have anything about me? I thought.

"Could I listen to the news before I go in?"

"Let me get it for you," he said and disappeared underneath. About five minutes later, he was back with a handheld radio which he promptly handed to me. I turned it on and started moving through the dial.

"VOV-1 News. 2145-1700," he said.

I dialed in and immediately heard the familiar rhythms of my native language. They were giving a report about tourism in Ha Long Bay and how its development had helped establish five new schools for some of the poorer districts of Quang Ninh province. The tone sounded for the top of the hour, and the news began.

"This is the Voice of Vietnam News. The town of Thai Nguyen is still reeling from the tragic death of its head councilman Dr. Nguyen Ton Duc, who was found beaten to death in his office at the Thai Nguyen People's Council Building. The motive behind Dr. Duc's murder appears to be robbery as the safe in his office was opened and an undisclosed amount of cash belonging to the People's Council is missing. The widow of Dr. Duc spoke to the media for the first time earlier today. 'There are no words to describe my heartbreak. Duc was a loving husband and a wonderful father. He was a family man at heart. He *cared deeply about the people of Thai Nguyen. In my opinion, this was a carefully planned robbery by a group of professionals, who knew his habits and took advantage of the peoples' servant.' Police spokesman Ngo Dang says they are looking into some criminal gangs in Thai Nguyen, who may have had a hand in this brutal killing. In the meantime, you can pay your respects to the family of Dr. Duc as his body will lie in state at the provincial People's Council building later today starting at 10 AM. This is the Voice of Vietnam."*

I switched it off. My head spun wildly, but my face remained expressionless and everyone who had gathered around to listen looked at me. I handed the radio back to the sailor and went and stood at the railing. They would cover-up the truth to save everyone the embarrassment of the affair. This meant one thing; they would not be coming after me. A gust of wind whipped through my shortened hair. It felt like the gust of freedom. On the horizon, the morning sun was just beginning to paint its colors lifting the darkness which had hung over me. The glory of life once again bolstered its claim on my soul. I felt free. I looked up into the heavens.

"Thank you, God."

Part III

Under the Banana Tree

Second Point of Contact

"Martin. I just saw the first lightening bug of the season," my mom said.

Lightening bugs start illuminating the night around dusk of late spring.

"All right. I'll check them out front."

The open front door allowed a beautifully cool breeze to permeate the house. As I reached the screen door, I noticed a girl standing out on the street holding something in her hand and looking at our mail box. I watched her for a moment. She had long black hair, and she was Asian. I watched as she touched her fingers to the letters of the mail box. The front door screeched as I opened it, and she immediately looked up at me and took two steps back like she was ready to run.

"Can I help you?"

She just looked and said nothing. And then I noticed who it really was. It was that girl I saw in Hanoi at the ice cream shop or possibly the girl I saw at Returned Sword Lake cuddled on the bench with her lover. It may have been that girl on page 89 in the book by my bed stand or the girl I grabbed a hold of in Thai Nguyen; it was definitely the girl that smiled at my dad under the banana tree. My heart froze in fear. What was she doing here? She started walking away.

"No, wait," I said and walked down the porch steps. "Wait. Can I help you?"

She stopped for a moment then turned around and walked over and stood beside the mail box. I towered two steps above her on the sidewalk which stretched from the porch.

"Are you Martin Kinney?" she said in excellent English, pointing at the name on the mail box.

"Yes, well, that Martin Kinney was my father. I'm Martin Kinney Jr."

She stood like an angel wearing a white blouse and blue jeans. My heart pounded. It had to be the girl from the book on page 89.

"I'm sorry," she said and handed me the plastic card that she had been holding.

"What?"

I reached out and took it. It was my old driver's license.

"I'm sorry," she said again.

"What? How?"

Then I looked at her face again.

"It's you. You're the one who stole my wallet. I grabbed your arm that day at the festival. It's you."

"I'm sorry," she said for one last time and then started walking up the street.

"Do you know how much trouble that caused me?" I said instinctively. I jumped down the two steps onto the road. "I had nothing. I ... Hey, come back here. Hey!"

She continued walking up Home Avenue. I wallowed in my anger for another few moments until I realized that perhaps I just made the biggest mistake of my life. Why would she go completely out of her way to return a stolen license three years from the date of the incident? I also realized that the girl I had been dreaming about for a long time stood on my street in Lyndora, and all I could do is yell at her.

Slick Martin. Slick.

I started running after her.

"Wait. No wait. I'm sorry. I didn't mean to get angry. Wait."

She continued walking away from me undeterred.

"Please," I said.

She stopped. I caught up to her and stood directly behind her.

"Thank you. Thank you for bringing back my license. You must have gone well out of your way."

I touched her gently on her right arm.

"Really. Thank you."

She turned her face around towards me, and I noticed she was crying.

"Oh. No. What's wrong? Don't cry."

She turned away again.

"Come on. Can we sit on the steps out front and talk? It's okay. Can we talk?"

She nodded her head and turned around. We walked back to the house in complete silence. Several lightning bugs flew by and my eyes trailed after them.

"Let's sit here," I said, pointing to the top step right beside the mail box.

She sat daintily down on my right side. My wide girth

wouldn't quite fit on the remaining portion of the cement step so half of me used the cool grass as an overflow.

"So," I said, breaking the silence although I didn't know how to proceed from there. "It's a cool evening."

"Yes."

"I'm curious. Why did you bring me back my license?"

"I don't know."

A lightning bug flew right in front of me. I stood up and stumbled down the small bank cupping my hands trying to catch it.

"Come here, come here. Got it."

I carried the bug over in my cupped hands.

"Look," I said lifting up one side of my hand. "Isn't it beautiful?"

She looked inside as the lightning bug blinked twice illuminating my palms.

"Yes."

"When I was a boy, I used to spend every summer evening out here catching these things. I put them in jars with holes punched out in the top. I'd let them go before I went to bed. I'd catch them again the next night."

"It sounds like a wonderful way to grow up."

"Hardly. My dad was always drunk and my Mom, well, she's a unique one too. I tried to stay out of the house as much as possible."

"When you came to Vietnam, you went for your father, didn't you?"

I looked at her in disbelief.

"How would you know that?"

"My English teacher in Thai Nguyen was a friend of your friend. He saw your license that I had on my key chain and started talking about you."

"What? Wait, you mean Jason?"

"Yes, that was his name. Mr. Jason."

"You know him? Is that why you came here?"

"No, I don't know him. I told him I found your wallet and that I kept your license as a good luck charm."

"Whoa. This is unbelievable. Yeah, Jason saved me. I didn't have any money and I didn't know what to do," I paused trying to grasp the situation. "You met Jason?"

"I'm sorry," she said again and turned away from me.

"No, don't. That's all in the past. What did he tell you about my father?"

"Nothing."

"No, really," I insisted.

"He told me that you came to Vietnam to bury your father's ashes. That he had been a soldier in the war."

I nodded my head. I had never met this girl before, but I felt like I had been dreaming about her for three years. This was my banana tree moment. I was sure she would leave after tonight and I would never see her again, but for now, for this moment, the girl who smiled at me continued to sit beside me.

"I was only in Vietnam for three days, but it changed my life. Actually, I should probably thank you."

She looked at me in a startled manner. The breeze blew her hair softly to the left. My heart pounded as if I had just walked up a steep hill. I also felt out of breath. Love is the most rigorous type of exercise.

"Thank me? Why? I stole your wallet."

"If you hadn't stolen my wallet, I never would have experienced Hanoi with Jason and my taxi driver Tan like I did. I never would have experienced their kindness – their generosity. Those three days changed my life. I also wouldn't be talking with you right now."

"How can you thank me?" she said with a hint of disbelief and almost anger. "I would believe you more if you were angry at me."

"Believe me, I'm not angry."

There was silence for a moment.

"You must have loved your father to do that for him."

I laughed. Oh, the irony.

"That's the strange thing. I hated my father. He was mean to me and horrible to live with. But when he was dying, he asked me to do this for him, and I couldn't refuse. Strangely, by following his wishes, it changed me for the better."

There was another awkward pause.

"So was it?" I asked.

"Was what?"

"Was my license lucky for you?" I asked with a smile.

"It saved my life."

"How did it save your life?"

"It's a long story."

"I've got nothing to do. Trust me. I have absolutely nothing to do."

It wasn't Tuesday after all.

"We could go for a walk if you like. I'd love to hear your story."

"Okay. I'd like that."

"But wait, I don't even know your name."

"I am My Phuong."

"My Phuong," I repeated. "Did you say 'Phuong'?"

"No, it's Phuong. Short, hard tone."

"Phuong."

"Yes, that's right."

"Like the flower?"

"Yes, that's right. You know about the Phuong flower?" she asked surprised.

I stood up immediately and held up my finger for her to wait for a minute.

"Wait right here. Can you wait right here for one minute?"

She nodded.

"I mean, if I go in the house and come out in one minute, you'll still be here?"

"Yes. I'll wait."

"Promise?"

"Yes, I promise. I'm not going anywhere," she said as she smiled at me.

She smiled at me. That smile ripped through my stomach. I didn't know what it meant, but there it was. That smile, and it was directed at me. I couldn't bear leaving her, but I did. I ran into the house, through the kitchen, up the stairs, into my bedroom, and grabbed the Vietnam book from my night stand. I flew down the stairs sounding to myself like a herd of elephants, through the kitchen out the door and I noticed immediately that she was still there. My heart sighed in relief. I went down the steps, across the sidewalk and plopped down beside her. My body crashed into hers as I sat down and she went flying two feet in the opposite direction.

Gosh, I'm the most awkward person in the world, I thought.

"Sorry."

"Not at all," she said with her proper English.

"Here," I handed her the picture book. "Turn to page 89."

Her delicate hands slowly flipped through the pages until she stopped on page 89. Her face lit up immediately.

"Oh, the Phuong flower," she said picking up the petals in her hand. "It's still so beautiful."

"It was my only souvenir from Vietnam because I didn't have any money."

Her face turned sour.

"No—Not that, no. I didn't mean that. I mean, it is the best souvenir I ever could have gotten with all the money in the world."

"It's travelled all this way, and it is still very beautiful," she said.

I hesitated to say it, but I had to.

"Just like you."

She looked up at me and smiled again.

"So you have kept this flower in this book for three years?"

"Yes. I can't tell you how many times I got out this book and stared at the flower to remember my time in Vietnam or to remember my dad. Or just to look at the girl on page 89," I said. I wished I could have erased that last comment.

"You think she is beautiful?"

"Yes," I said. "But not as beautiful as you."

I wanted to kick myself for saying that too. I nervously grabbed the book from her.

"I'll just put this on the porch, and then we can go for that walk. You can tell me about how lucky my license is."

"Okay."

I ran to the porch, plopped the book on the swing, and then we started walking down Home Avenue – a large round, red-headed American and a petite Asian. Several neighbors greeted us with 'Hello' as they looked curiously on. We walked down to Main and then over to Hansen Avenue. Then we walked down past the bowling alley, up the steps which led to my old alma mater – Butler High School – across the road and within an hour we were sitting in a pavilion at Alameda Park. She told me about Hung who pushed me, and Hoa, and Co Thu. She told me about Mr. Duc's shave and then the English lessons she gave him. She told me all about the affair, the visit from Mrs. Duc, and how she took the license and plunged it into Mr. Duc's eye. She told me about how she killed him and how she escaped to Haiphong. She told me about the small room in the container and how she listened to the shortwave radio to hear about her freedom.

I sat completely shocked at everything she endured.

"My Phuong, I don't even know what to say. It's unbelievable."

My life seemed easy compared to hers.

"I survived," she said.

"I'm so sorry My Phuong. How long ago was all of that?"

"About a year and a half."

"What happened since then? How did you end up at my house in Lyndora?"

She turned away from me and walked over to the edge of the kids' playground. There was a small, metal merry-go-round that twirled willing victims, the kind that made me sick to my stomach. She sat on the edge of it and gave it one twirl. I watched her go around. She smiled as she went by. She had such a playful, youthful flare. She put her feet down to stop in front of me and stood up.

"I'm sorry. Am I asking too many questions? You don't need to tell me anything if you don't want."

"No. I want to. When the freighter arrived in the Port of Los Angeles, we had to remain in the container for about twelve hours. Finally, one of the guys showed up and sneaked us out of the ship through the shipyard and into a van. We were transported to downtown LA and were told we had to work for three years to pay off our passage to America even though I had already paid way more than originally told. There was a group of leaders, Asian and Mexican, and they threatened us with all kinds of things if we gave them trouble or tried to escape. So I worked in a factory in downtown LA for over a year. They kept a close eye on us, and since I didn't have any papers, I basically just did whatever they said."

"Did they mistreat you? Did they hurt you or make you do things you didn't want?"

"It was fine, Martin. They didn't make me do anything I wasn't used to."

"What happened?"

"The INS raided the place about three months ago. We were put into a detention center until we could be processed. I claimed asylum and eventually when I told them my story, they granted it to me. That was two weeks ago. They gave me my possessions, which were few. Your license was still there. After all this time, I still had your license. My parents had always taught me not to steal, and I know they would have been disappointed with me. So I thought I would go and give it to you as the first step of starting my new life."

My heart raged for this poor girl. I didn't want to ask her what her plans were next. I couldn't bear the thought that she would leave.

We walked back towards Lyndora and just chatted about random things. We stopped at Wendy's and I bought her a burger. I had a triple. She ate about half of it and gave me the rest. We laughed and smiled. It was the most magical night of my life. We arrived back at Home Avenue and took a seat on that same familiar step. I was still halfway into the grass. The screen door opened.

"Martin, where the hell have you been? It's almost eleven o'clock. Who's out there with you?"

"Mom, this is My Phuong."

"Who's that?"

"Hello," My Phuong said to my mother. "Nice to meet you."

"Martin, you need to come in now. It's cold out there."

She completely ignored My Phuong's gesture and just stared at her. I wanted nothing more than for her to go away.

"Mom, don't be so rude. She said 'hello' to you."

My Mom nodded to My Phuong insincerely.

"Come in now, Martin."

"Mom, stop treating me like a child. I'm trying to have a conversation here."

"What are you? Are you Asian?" my Mom said in the most embarrassing of manners.

"She's from Vietnam, Mom."

"Vietnam! Martin!"

"Mom, go inside."

The screen door slammed.

"My Phuong, I am so sorry. My mother had no right to treat you like that. But that's how my mother is. I'm sorry."

"Maybe I should go."

"Where? Where will you go?"

"I'll find a place."

"You mean you have no place to stay?" I asked.

"No, but don't worry. I'll find a place."

"No, My Phuong. You can stay here. We have plenty of room."

"No, I couldn't."

"Sure you can. There's an extra bedroom in the basement, and—"

"No, your mother doesn't like me."

"My mother doesn't like anyone."

"No, Martin I have to go."

She stood up and walked down the two steps to the road and then started to leave.

"My Phuong, please don't. I mean, if you want to leave … if you don't want to see me again, I understand, but …"

Perhaps there were tears in my eyes. I'm not sure, but I felt my heart breaking. I had been waiting for her for three years and the thought of her leaving tore me up.

"Oh, Martin. You have been so kind to me already. I just don't want to cause you any problems with your mother."

"But you need a place to stay, don't you?"

She looked away from me, and then turned her head back towards me and nodded.

"I have an idea. Do you trust me?"

"I trust you more than I've trusted anyone in a long time."

That made me smile immensely.

The Real Story of *My Phuong*

We walked down Home Avenue onto Main and continued down two blocks until we stood in front of Reverend Fox's parsonage.

"Where are we going, Martin?"

"Here. This is the home of Reverend Fox. I think he could help you."

"This is a church. No, Martin. No. I have to go."

She started walking the other way.

"My Phuong, what is it? Where will you go? My Phuong? Please, wait."

She stopped.

"Martin, not the church. I can't."

"What's the matter? Reverend Fox is really nice. I think he can help you."

She looked distressed, but eventually nodded and turned back to me.

"It's okay," I said and we both walked up his sidewalk towards his front door. A light burned dimly in the front room. I walked up the two cinderblock steps and knocked. After a few seconds, the aging Reverend Fox came to the door.

"Hello? Martin, how are you?"

"Reverend Fox, I'm really sorry to bother you this late at night. I'm wondering if you might be able to help us."

"Please come in. Come in."

"Reverend Fox, this is my friend My Phuong. She's from Vietnam."

"Pleasure to meet you."

"Hello sir," she replied.

"Please have a seat."

My Phuong and I sat down in a love seat. I brushed right up against her arm in a wonderfully intimate way.

"Sorry to bother you this late, but I'm wondering if you can help us."

"What is it Martin," the Reverend said as he sat down in a rocker but leaned forward toward us.

"My Phuong is a refugee from Vietnam. She has recently been granted asylum because of someone who had kept her in bondage unlawfully. Now she needs a place to stay for a few days until she can figure out what she is going to do. I remembered the apartment over your garage. You don't think—"

"Oh Martin, she is more than welcome to stay there. It's not completely clean, but—"

"No," My Phuong said abruptly. "That's not the reason why they gave me asylum."

"Oh," said Reverend Fox. "What is your story?"

I looked at her strangely trying to determine what she meant.

"I was raised a Protestant, like you," she said looking at the Reverend. "My father was a pastor in the south of Vietnam. In the highlands. You see, I'm not actually

Vietnamese. I am part of the *Mnong* ethnic group of Vietnam. My mother was half Vietnamese and they gave me a Vietnamese name hoping that I would be able to fit into society better when I was older."

"No, wait," I said interrupting her. "But you are from Thai Win. Thai Win is where you stole my wallet."

Reverend Fox looked quickly at me in apparent curiosity.

"No. I'm not from Thai Nguyen. I'm from Tay Nguyen – the central highlands, Dak Lak province, just outside of Buon Me Thuot."

I sat back in the couch astounded by the revelation. She was from Tay Nguyen. I thought of my dad.

"My father pastored a small church not too far from the provincial capital. It was not an official church. The local authorities would not allow us to build a real church, so we met in a longhouse of one of our member's family."

"I have heard that the church in Vietnam has been persecuted in many terrible ways," said the Reverend.

She nodded, and then continued her story.

"My father had worked hard for many years. He saw many converts, and the church grew to about sixty individuals. One week, about four years ago, we were planning a Saturday morning church picnic on one of the beautiful mountain tops. Everything was coordinated, and we were encouraged to invite some of our non-Christian friends. We arrived at the location around ten in the morning, and started singing and worshipping. Around eleven, we started a fire that we planned to cook our lunch over. It was a beautiful day. At around 11:15, we heard several cars pulling up, and we were surprised to see the police. Seven different police cars and three lorries. All of the congregation panicked and started to say things like we should all run away. But my father, he just stood there and told everyone that we were doing nothing wrong and that we should stay calm."

"I don't understand," I said. "Why were the police coming to a picnic?"

"In Vietnam, you have to have official permission from the government if you want to have a church meeting or any assembly of a large group."

"Why?"

"They think that we will try to subvert the government or something like that. So the police came and confronted my father. He stood in front of them and said that they were doing nothing wrong. The police accused him of breaking the law and said that he would have to come with them. He agreed and started going towards the lorry."

My Phuong stopped talking, and I could see the tears forming in the corners of her eyes.

"Then one of the officers started yelling at him. He grabbed one of the burning branches from the fire and poked it into my father's face. My father screamed in pain and several men from our congregation came towards him to aid him. That's when the police came at the crowd in full force. They started beating men, women and children. One man was thrown into the fire and severely burned. Others scattered through the woods."

The Reverend had pulled out a handkerchief and rubbed his eyes. I used my sleeve. I couldn't comprehend the amount of suffering My Phuong had experienced in her life.

"They arrested both of my parents. I ran down

through the trees to escape. I hid out in the forest for several hours and then finally made the three hour trek by foot back to my home. When I got there, everything was ransacked. Everything was smashed and destroyed. I sat in the corner that night and wept for about twelve hours until the next morning."

"You poor child," said Reverend Fox.

"I went to my Uncle's house in the morning, and he was gone too. The police had come to take him away that night. My Aunt was there, so we waited for three days to get any word about my parents. I couldn't take it any longer, so I went to Buon Me Thuot. I knew this was not very smart, but I didn't want to live without my parents. I marched right into the People's Council building, and demanded that they tell the police to release my parents. Some guards tried to remove me, but I yelled and made a scene. Finally, one of the officials came out of his office and motioned for them to let me through. He told me he would make a call and find out about them. I sat down and waited, and finally he came out and said without remorse 'They're dead.' I staggered out of there in shock. I wandered all the way back to my Aunt's longhouse, a four hour walk, without remembering anything other than what he told me. I wanted to die, and even tried to kill myself once. But more than anything else, I was angry at God. Reverend, how could God have let this happen to me? How could God allow something like this to happen to my parents?"

She broke down and cried. I lifted my arm up as if I was going to comfort her, but I was too afraid to touch her. She wiped her eyes with the Reverend's handkerchief.

"I don't know, My Phuong. I don't know," replied Reverend Fox.

"Reverend, I'm sorry. I didn't mean to," she stood up and put her hand on her forehead. "I don't know why I'm telling you all this."

"Because you need to. It's okay. We're your friends," replied Reverend Fox calmly.

She sat back down. I kept looking down at the floor. I had absolutely nothing to say.

"I turned away from my faith, and I ran away north, to Hanoi. I wanted nothing to do with God or the Vietnamese government. I hated them both. So I got involved in many different terrible things, just trying to forget who I was and where I came from. After a few months, I ended up in Thai Nguyen where I stole Martin's wallet."

"I did hear about the stolen wallet story. But this is quite an unexpected ending to it."

"This is why I was given asylum in America. Religious persecution. I have been given a new life in America because of a religion I don't even believe in anymore."

Reverend Fox seemed to ponder the gravity of her situation perhaps wanting to choose his words carefully.

"My Phuong, I can't even begin to imagine that I understand what you have gone through in your life because I can't. I can't even tell you why you suffered the way you have. All I can tell you is that you are loved. And you have friends here who want to help you. I would be honored to give you the apartment over the garage to stay in. It's not much, but you can stay there as long as you need in order to figure out your next step."

"No, I don't want to be a burden. I'll be all right."

"My Phuong, please stay," I said to her. They were my first words in several minutes.

She looked up at me, and then over at Reverend Fox.

"Okay. Thank you."

The Reverend got together some blankets and toiletries and then we all three walked up the steps to the garage apartment. He tidied up a few things and gave her some instructions concerning the apartment's peculiarities. Then he told her that he would be in the house if she needed anything. We all three walked down the steps and stood in the front lawn near the driveway where my dad made his terrible scene many years ago. As the Reverend said goodnight and turned toward his house, My Phuong ran over to him and hugged him. She then turned back around and came and stood beside me.

"Thank you Martin. I don't know how to thank you. Your pastor is a really sweet man."

"He's not even my pastor. I don't go to church."

"How do you know him?"

"It's a long story that I'll have to tell you sometime."

"I hope so. Maybe tomorrow?"

"Sure, maybe tomorrow. Goodnight," I said and turned to walk home.

"Martin," she said. "Thank you."

"For what? I didn't do anything."

"Yes, you did?"

"I had no idea what happened to your family. I'm so—"

"Shhh," she said and walked over to me, looking up at my large frame.

"Martin?"

"Yes?"

"Can you lean over a little?"

I leaned over toward her, and she goose necked up and kissed me on the cheek.

"Goodnight."

She turned, walked up to Reverend Fox's old apartment and closed the door behind her. The irony of everything flooded my emotions. In some ways, I was travelling the same footsteps as dad, but I only hoped to do it better.

I staggered home, barely 'touching the ground' which was quite a feat at my weight. I was seriously in love.

Mom in the Morning

First thing in the morning, I went out to the front porch to retrieve the Vietnam book that I left on the swing. It wasn't there. I went back into the house, and Mom was just then descending from her upstairs bedroom.

"Mom, where is that book that I left on the porch last night?"

"I threw it in the trash."

"What?"

"We don't need any books about Vietnam in this house. That subject is painful enough," she said as she walked by me into the kitchen.

"Mom, you had no right. That was my book. You just don't throw things out without asking me."

"Martin, that was your father's book. I hadn't seen that in years. We just don't need it around here."

"Where did you throw it?"

"Martin, just leave it be."

"Mom," I said sternly.

"It's in the bin on the back porch."

I rushed out and opened the lid of the metal trash can and found it lying on top. I picked it up and immediately turned to page 89 to secure my flower. It wasn't there. I flipped through the nearby pages but found nothing. Then I flipped through the whole book, eventually grabbing it by the spine and shaking it violently upside down waiting for the fan-shaped flower to flutter out. Nothing. I opened the screen door to the kitchen and leaned inside.

"Mom, did you see a red flower in the book?"

"Yes, it fell out when I picked the book up. I threw it in the burn trash."

I came back inside and immediately went to the inside trash can which had papers and consumables which we burnt out back.

"I burnt it last night Martin. It's gone."

I stood flatfooted. My heart descended into that familiar place full of despair and hatred. The place where I often hid to pretend I didn't belong to this family. My souvenir was gone. The gift from Tan, the symbol of my Vietnamese woman, the Phuong flower was gone. I ran outside to the back corner of our yard where we had a metal burn barrel. Burning trash in Lyndora had long been illegal, but my parents never did get out of the habit. I picked up a stick and rummaged through the ashes, but there was no sign of red, no sign of the flower – nothing but a pile of ashes. I rubbed my arms against my head motioning for something to strike out at. Anger. It boiled inside. I couldn't stay in this house any longer. I had been trapped here for thirty-nine years. But this was it. I threw the stick into the trees and marched into the house.

"Mom. I've had it. I can't live here anymore."

"Martin, what has gotten into you?"

"You throw my book in the trash, you burn my flower," I realized how petty it all sounded.

"Martin, stop talking like a child. It was just a flower."

"That's just it, Mom. It wasn't just a flower. It meant something to me. And stop treating me like a child. I thought that after Dad had died that we would be able to get along and live like a normal family. But it's no different. You are still treating me like I am a teenager. You are treating me like I have no wants or desires of my own. You just expect me to work at K-Mart and bowl on Tuesdays. There's more to me than that. Can't you see that? Can't you see that?"

My mom looked startled. She put down her cereal spoon, stood up and walked towards me.

"Martin, of course I want you to be happy."

"Then stay out of my life."

"Martin, you don't mean that."

"Yes, yes I do."

I backed away from her.

"I'm going to find my own place."

"Martin, don't be silly. You can't afford your own place. It makes no sense when you can live here for free."

"You're wrong Mom. Living here is not free. Not at all."

"Martin, no. I forbid you to leave this house. I need you here."

"Mom, why can't you understand that I am a thirty-nine year old adult?"

"Does this have something to do with that Vietnamese girl who was here last night?"

"No, it has nothing to do with her."

"Who was she?"

"Oh no. She is off limits, Mom."

"Off limits, huh? Is there something going on there, Martin? You couldn't possibly dream of getting to know a girl like that."

"Like what?"

"You can't get involved with those floozy Asian girls. That's what got in your dad's head and messed him all up."

"Mom, we are not having this conversation," I said as I started to walk away.

"Martin, I just want what is best for you. You aren't going to see her again, are you?"

I turned around and said emphatically, "Yes, yes I am. I'm going to see her today. I hope to see her tomorrow. I hope I see her every day for the rest of my life."

"Martin," my Mother said flaring her eyes at me. "I don't ever want to see her here again. Do you hear me?"

"As long as I live here, I can bring home whomever I like," I said in an irritated and disrespectful manner. I turned my back on her, went to the phone, and dialed work. "Mr. Hutchings. Yes, this is Martin. I'm not going to be able to make work today. Yes, that's right. I'm coming down with something. Yes, sir. Okay. I'll see you tomorrow."

My mom immediately came into the living room.

"Martin, you can't skip work."

"Yes, I can. I have more important things to do. I have to go see My Phuong," I said and stormed up the steps to my room to get ready to leave.

"Martin, Martin!" she yelled after me, but I did my best to ignore her, and I slammed the door just to let her know that I would not listen to her.

Day Two

In the three years since I had visited Vietnam, I had actually accomplished a lot. I bought a computer and got connected to the Internet. I tried to get in touch with Jason and Tan in Vietnam, but unfortunately I had lost all of their contact information. But I spent a lot of time on the web reading about Southeast Asia – especially Vietnam. I had first become curious at looking at images of Vietnamese girls – looking for that beautiful face that I saw so many times when I was there. But over time, I found myself learning about the culture, people and places of the region. One of the things that fascinated me was the Khmer Rouge of Cambodia. They declared a 'Year Zero' when they took control of Cambodia in 1975 announcing that history was nothing and that their entire society was starting over from the beginning. In many ways, that is how I felt about my life. I was now on 'Day Two'. It was day two of My Phuong being a part of my life. Everything that happened to me in the past didn't matter anymore. I had a clean slate, and I intended to use it. In some ways, I agonized greatly that first morning, hoping more than anything that she would still be in Reverend Fox's apartment. I hoped beyond hope that she would not once again disappear like a vapor in a crowd.

At 10:15, I stood at the top of the steps over the Reverend Fox's garage and knocked delicately at My Phuong's door. There was no sound. I knocked again, and my heart leapt when I finally heard rustling from within and then footsteps. My Phuong opened the door. She had not left me.

"Good morning."

"Good morning, Martin."

"I'm sorry if I'm bothering you. I hope I didn't wake you up."

"No, not at all. I had just showered and dressed, and I was thinking about what to do today. Come in."

"Did you sleep okay?"

"Yes, I slept very well, thank you."

She wore a pair of jeans and a tight-fitting white turtle-neck blouse with long sleeves. I looked at her in adoration.

"How about you, Martin? Did you sleep well?" she asked.

"Ah," I hemmed and hawed around. "Well, okay I guess."

"Martin, do you have to work today?"

"No, I took the day off."

"Why did you do that?"

"I just wanted to be available to help you. I just came to help you."

She smiled.

"You've been a big help already."

"I want to be a bigger help. I want to," I then realized

how foolish I must have sounded. I needed to back down some. "So, what is it that you need to do?"

"I just have to figure out what my new life will be like."

I knew what I wanted her new life to be like. I wanted us to be together. But I could never say anything like that. Deep in my heart, I knew this could never be – not someone like her with someone like me – but hope doesn't stop at plausible possibilities. It plows through unchartered territory. Hope builds a home at the highest peak and then watches to see if it will come to fruition. I couldn't dare let on what I had in my heart. I sat in a chair and she sat across from me on the couch. We were silent for a few moments.

"I had a fight with my Mom this morning."

"Really? What happened?"

"You know that flower? The Phuong flower?"

She nodded.

"Well, she burnt it, and it made me really mad."

"Why did she burn it?"

"That's what she does. She destroys things. That was my only souvenir from Vietnam, and now it's gone."

There was a long pause of silence. We both started talking at the same time.

"You go," I said.

"No, what were you going to say?"

"My taxi driver, Tan, he said that that flower represented the Vietnamese woman that I didn't meet because I didn't have any money."

I laughed to myself, and she looked over at me with a sweet smile.

"Because of that mean person who stole your wallet?"

"That's right. He said no Vietnamese girl for me because I was broke."

"Well," she said in a flirtatious manner. "There is still one Phuong in your life."

She smiled at me again. I must have turned beat red at that remark. I had no idea how to interpret it, or what it really meant. A Phuong in my life. What did that mean? If hope had been sitting at the earth's highest peak, it had just hitched a ride on a rocket to the upper stratosphere. I had to change the subject. If I was misinterpreting her banter, I didn't want to know about it. At least not now.

"So I know that Phuong means flower—"

"Phuong," she repeated emphasizing the heavy tone.

"Phuong. Sorry. So what does *My* mean?"

"Well, *My* means aesthetic. It comes from the Chinese character Mei."

"Aesthetic?" I looked at her blankly.

"Yes, like beauty or beautiful," she clarified.

"Beautiful," I repeated.

She paused for a second.

"But that is not the only meaning, do you know that *My* also means American?"

"No, really? Your name means American?"

"Yes, it's true. Beautiful and American are the same word."

"Why is that?"

"Well, I heard the story that Vietnamese always liked the American flag and thought it looked very beautiful. And actually, the stars look like flowers. A field of flowers. Beautiful Americans."

She laughed.

"Americans can be pretty ugly too," I said with a smile.

"No, I like Americans."

"No, don't say that. That's what my taxi driver Tan would say. 'Americans are fat. Hey, Martin, why don't you wear short pants? Because you too fat? Right? But don't worry, I like Americans.'"

We both laughed out loud. It was the most fun I had in a long time, or at least since last evening – Day One. Perhaps it was the most fun I ever had. I wanted to bottle this moment and keep it forever. I couldn't even breathe. She just sat there so beautiful, so kind, and so easy to talk to.

"And Phuong means flower. So your name means beautiful flower."

"Or American flower," she said, with a hint of devil's play.

"That's right. Or how about 'Beautiful American flower'?"

She laughed again.

"Yes, but you know Phuong has another meaning as well."

"What's that?"

"Phoenix."

"Huh?"

"Phoenix."

"Like the city? Phoenix, Arizona?" I asked.

"Yes, it's the same as that, but it means the bird. Phoenix the bird."

I had a blank stare on my face.

"Phoenix is a bird in ancient mythology that at the end of its life burns up, but then out of the ashes rises another Phoenix bird."

I really didn't learn much in school. I realized that.

"So your name means 'Beauty rising out of the ashes'?"

Beauty rising. There were no other words to describe her life or my feelings. I marveled at this beautiful creature sitting beside me. It was too good to be true. Now I knew how my dad felt under the banana trees. A war zone all around and a piece of heaven suddenly comes into your life.

We chatted in a light-hearted manner until around noon when Reverend Fox came to invite us for a light lunch at his house. I ate very carefully and very little. I wanted to lose weight like I never wanted to before. Perhaps if I was thinner she would be attracted to me. I would do anything for her. I would never eat again if she asked me. Reverend Fox gave her some advice about possibly finding a job in the area. She seemed very open to the possibility, and I told her that I could help her that afternoon look around at some possibilities.

On Day Three, I called off work again and took My Phuong around Butler applying for various jobs at restaurants and retail stores. On Day Four, I took My Phuong for a second round of applications, and then we ended up having a picnic lunch at Moraine State Park in the afternoon. On Day Five, I told my manager Mr. Hutchins that I had pneumonia and might be out for a while. I spent the day re-canvassing retail shops on Main Street in Butler. I took her out for dinner at Natilli's where she ordered spaghetti and a bottle of wine of which she drank the whole thing. On the way home, she was quite drunk, and I helped her up the steps and put a blanket on her as she lay down on the couch. She drifted off to sleep in a drunken slumber, and I watched her for several minutes. I could have sat and pondered her beauty all night, but I knew it was not right. I wrote a note for her and placed it on the end table by the couch. 'You are sleeping peacefully. It looks like the wine did you in for the night. I hope you have sweet dreams. See you in the morning. Martin.' I debated for a long time whether to add the word 'love' or not. Eventually, I decided that I couldn't do it.

I slept horribly that night thinking constantly of her sleeping peacefully on her couch. I had the terrible feeling that everything I was doing would only end in more heartbreak, but I had no other options. I would do anything for her, and if I ended up getting hurt, well, at least I still had Day One through Day Five.

On Day Six, I didn't even call in sick. They expected me to be out for a few more days. I wondered if I would ever go back to work. Mom would yell at me every morning and threaten to call K-Mart and tell them that I played hooky. But she never did. So on Day Six, I arrived at My Phuong's apartment around 9:30. She was cooking in the kitchen when I knocked on the front door.

"Martin, come in," she said enthusiastically. "I'm making you breakfast."

"You are making me breakfast?"

"Yes. I have eggs, and I walked down to 7-11 and got a package of sausage. I hope you like it. Oh, and I have some orange juice and toast."

She was an angel from God. I was sure of it.

She talked non-stop as she made my breakfast. I marveled at every word she said and at ever movement she made.

"Eat!"

"It looks delicious."

"Eat. And if you don't eat a lot, I'll be very offended. Vietnamese people believe that if guests don't eat much, they don't like the food. So I hope you like it."

"It looks wonderful."

"So prove it," she said with a smirk on her face.

I did. I ate four eggs, five pieces of toast, twelve sausages, and three glasses of orange juice. I couldn't help myself. I ate like I never ate before. She sat across from me and kept encouraging me to eat more and more. I finished my plate and she added more onto it. Finally, she ran out of food and fretted that I didn't have enough. I told her I was never so full in my life and it was the best breakfast ever. She smiled at me again.

"All week, you haven't been eating very much. I'm worried that you are losing weight," she said. "Have you been afraid to eat around me?"

I put my head down slightly and nodded.

"Why?"

I just shook my head and smiled, but I refused to say anything.

"Why?" she persisted.

"I ..."

"Why Martin?"

"I've been trying to lose weight."

"Why are you trying to lose weight?"

I didn't say anything again.

"Martin, tell me. Why have you been trying to lose weight?"

This was the moment I had been trying to avoid all week. I didn't want to come clean with my true feelings because I felt that everything would come to an end.

"Martin. Why have you been trying to lose weight? And Martin, why haven't you gone to work at all this week?"

I looked down at the ground for a few seconds, and then I turned back into her face.

"I haven't gone to work this week so that I could spend time with you."

"But you could spend time after work, right?"

"I'm afraid if I go to work, then you will be gone."

She turned away from me for a minute and then persisted in her questioning.

"And the eating? Why haven't you been eating this week?"

I hesitated for a long time and then looked back at her again.

"I thought that if I could lose some weight, that maybe you could be attracted to me. That maybe you could look at me as ..." I stopped and looked down at the floor.

She reached over and touched my cheek and lifted my head so that we were eye-to-eye.

"Martin, you have been the kindest, sweetest person I have ever met. What would I have done without you? You have helped me so much. And Martin, I'm sorry I got drunk last night. Sometimes getting drunk is just my way of forgetting all the problems that I have in my life. But I woke up in the morning, and I realized that you tucked me in. You tucked me in. I have never had anyone tuck me in since I was a child living with my parents."

She turned away from me for a second and then turned back. Tears were streaming down her cheeks.

"And you didn't take advantage of me. You had every chance in the world to do whatever you wanted with me last night, but you are the first man to ever treat me with respect. I don't know how I could ever thank you."

I started crying as well.

"My Phuong. I know I'm fat, and I'm ugly. I'm not attractive, not like you."

"Martin, don't. You don't know the things I've done. You don't know."

"I don't care what you've done."

"Martin. I've been bad. Really bad. When I left Ban Me Thuot, I was angry at the world and I would do anything to survive. I lied; I stole; I became a Karaoke girl. I am not a clean person Martin. You don't know how bad I've been."

"I don't care about what you've done in the past. I really don't care. I don't care."

"But Martin—"

"My Phuong, I don't have anything to offer you. I don't have any money, I don't have a house, I don't have a good job, and I'm fat and ugly. That's all I have to offer you. But My Phuong, I love you. I love you so much it hurts, and I would treat you so well. And—"

"Oh, Martin. You are the sweetest man in the world."

She put her hands on each of my cheeks and rubbed my scraggly whiskers just staring at me for a minute. Then she smiled at me. She leaned over and put her hands around my neck and kissed me on the lips. I felt like our lips were connected for an eternity. Then she pulled back from me and smiled again.

"Martin, it's okay. You can go back to work tomorrow. I'm not going anywhere. China Buffet called this morning, and I start work there tomorrow afternoon."

I leaned back and just realized that the girl under the

banana tree truly smiled at me. I didn't know why she smiled, and I didn't know how long she would continue smiling, but I just knew that you didn't second guess instances like this – not in the hell-hole named Lyndora.

My Girl & My Mom

My Phuong continued to live in Reverend Fox's apartment. I continued to work at K-Mart but I had a new place I loved to stop for lunch – China Buffet. My Phuong wore the cutest blue uniform and would come around to fill up my cup and smile at me. Nothing else needed to be said. She was my girl. I had a girl. I had a hard time convincing myself that I had a girl, but there she was filling my tea cup at lunch and hanging out with me every evening.

Mom constantly harassed me about everything those days, and I kept planning to find a way to get my own place, but it just hadn't happened yet. Every evening I went over to My Phuong's place and we played games like little kids. She loved Uno, and we would play cut-throat for hours. Sometimes Reverend Fox would join us as well, and we would've woken up the neighbors with our hooting and hollering if it had been much later in the evening. We also watched a lot of TV. My Phuong loved to watch cooking shows and scratched down every recipe telling me over and over that she was going to make it for me. She would sit on my right with a beer in her hand. I would sit drinking my glass of milk constantly edging over to put my arm around her. Other days we just sat out on Reverend Fox's wooden picnic table and talked. On Wednesday evenings, we could hear the faint voices of the few church members singing hymns before their prayer meeting. I always wondered if those songs took her back to her childhood. I could never imagine how much her life had changed since the time when her father was a pastor and she sat in the church service singing hymns like that.

I left her about nine each evening, but before I did, she would kiss me – a cute peck on the lips. We hadn't quite figured out how to be physical with each other at that point, or at least I hadn't figured it out. I just didn't want to move too quickly and make a wrong move.

By the time summer officially commenced, we had been in this routine for about three weeks. Mom would typically be sitting on the porch when I came home. We didn't say much to each other those days other than about the trivial matters concerning living in the same house. I never told Mom where My Phuong lived. I don't know how she would have reacted to having My Phuong and me in that same apartment where the young Reverend and my Mom kindled their youthful passion.

One night after I pulled into the driveway and came up the front steps, Mom was waiting on the porch swing ready to ask me an unexpected question.

"Well, Martin? Are you ever going to let me meet this girl of yours?"

I hesitated. I never wanted my Mom near My Phuong, but I didn't want to tell her that.

"I didn't think you wanted to meet her."

"I do. I would like to meet her," she said, taking a drag on her cigarette.

"Mom, honestly, I don't know if that is a good idea," I said going back on my reservations about being frank.

"And why is that?"

"What are you going to say to her?"

"I just want to meet her."

"Don't do any of your silly business. Okay?" I warned her. "I don't want you to make her feel uncomfortable or unwanted. Will you treat her as a guest?"

"Martin, you have my word. I'll be a lady. Bring her for dinner tomorrow. We haven't eaten together for a while. I'll make a casserole."

"Okay. I'll bring her."

I dreaded the thought of bringing My Phuong home to meet my Mom, but it was about time. At lunch I informed My Phuong, and she seemed pleased that my Mom wanted to have her come. I wasn't so sure. I warned her that she would probably be offended, but My Phuong assured me that she could take it all. I had no reason to doubt her in the slightest. I believed she was the strongest woman in the world, and she would need every last fiber of that strength to withstand the hurricane that had the capability to attack at any moment.

My Phuong arrived at the house on foot around 7 PM. She wore black dress pants and a pretty pink sleeveless blouse. I loved looking at her walking towards me.

"Hi, My Phuong. Dinner is ready."

"Hi, Martin."

"Are you ready?"

"Yes. I'm ready," she said conveying a positive

attitude.

I smiled at her and opened the screen door leading her into the house. Mom was putting the finishing touches on the meal. A loaf of freshly baked bread sat on the table alongside a chicken and rice casserole. My Phuong's ethnicity no doubt had something to do with the rice.

"Mom," I said as we entered the kitchen. Mom stopped setting the table, quickly took off her apron and slightly grinned out of the side of her mouth. "This is My Phuong. My Phuong, this is my Mom. Mrs. Kinney."

"Martin, don't be so formal. She can call me Jane. Nice to meet you My Phuong – I'm sure I didn't say your name right."

They reached out to shake each other's hands.

"I am honored to meet you Jane."

"Here, My Phuong you sit here by me, and Martin sit on the end. Now what would you like to drink?"

"Oh, I'm not thirsty."

"Nonsense. Do you drink alcohol? Beer. How about beer? Do you like beer?"

"Yes, I do," My Phuong replied in the dainty polite way she had about her.

"Martin, get her a beer from the fridge."

"We don't have any beer in the fridge."

"Yes we do. Look in the back left. There's some in there."

"I don't need to have a beer," My Phuong said.

"Sure you do. Martin, get her one."

I reached into the fridge and found a cold one in the back, and set it down beside My Phuong.

"Martin, don't be so barbaric. Get her a glass and

open it for her.

I went to the utensil drawer to find a bottle opener.

"I sometimes wish Martin would just have a beer so he would relax a little bit and not be so uptight about everything. Don't you find Martin to be a little uptight sometimes?"

"I think Martin is very sweet," she looked at me and made me blush.

"Yes, of course, he's sweet," my mother said with a hint of sarcasm.

My Mom served us each a heaping spoonful of the casserole and passed around the bread and butter. She was a good cook when she took the time. She kept encouraging My Phuong to drink her beer and eat more of the casserole, but My Phuong remained very measured on both accounts.

"So, Martin says that you were a friend of a friend in Vietnam, is that true?"

My Phuong looked over at me as if to acknowledge the slight fudging I was doing to the truth.

"Yes, that's right. I came to visit a relative in America, and when I had a chance to come east, I thought I would look up Martin," she lied.

"And you just decided to stay?"

"Yes."

"Why?"

"Mom, do you have to ask so many questions?"

"Martin, you said I should try to get to know her. Well, I'm trying."

"It's okay," replied My Phuong. "I found that Lyndora is a nice place."

"Ha. That's a bunch of baloney. No one ever stays in

this crummy place. Except Martin, of course."

"Mom!"

"Now don't misunderstand me. If someone likes Lyndora and wants to stay, that's fine with me. It's just not very ordinary."

"The people are nice. And now that I have a job—"

"Yes, you are at the China Buffet, right?"

"Yes."

"Well, you must fit in real well there. I mean, you have the same language, don't you?"

"No, I speak Vietnamese, and they speak Chinese."

"I know that, but they are basically the same, right? It's all that choppy back and forth sounds. I can't make heads nor tails out of it. You can at least understand each other, right?"

"No. They are completely different. When my boss speaks Chinese, I can't understand anything."

"Is that right? Huh. Drink your beer."

"The food is very good," My Phuong replies.

"Oh, no, I'm sure you don't like it very well."

"No, I do, really."

"Yes, Mom. I like the bread."

She rolled her eyes at me.

"So where is it that you are staying?"

We were finally hitting dangerous waters.

"She's just rented an apartment not far from here," I quickly butted in.

"It's at the Methodist church. I rent an apartment from Reverend Fox."

"Reverend Fox?" she replied with a disgusted look on her face. She glared at me, and I could nearly feel the venom from her fangs.

"Yes, the one above his garage."

"Martin."

"Mom."

She stood up and went to the sink standing there for a moment.

"I'm okay. I just need a drink."

She poured herself a glass of bourbon, and then turned back around.

"Martin, get your guest another beer."

"No, ma'am. That's enough."

My Mom took another sip and then took a deep breath as if to compose herself.

"Well, I personally have never cared much for that Reverend Fox."

"He's been very nice to me."

"Perhaps he has. I just don't think he's the most sincere man in the world."

"Mom, can we just not do this?"

"Do what, Martin?"

My Phuong just looked straight ahead most likely wondering what was going on. I had purposely not told Mom about My Phuong's apartment because I knew it would bring up too many unnecessary memories. I also hadn't felt the need to tell My Phuong about my Mom's old fling with Reverend Fox. Mom finished her bourbon and poured herself another. We all sat quietly just eating for a few minutes. We finally got onto the topic of TV, and My Phuong relayed to my Mom her favorite shows none of which were favorites of my Mom.

When we had finished off the casserole, Mom brought over a chocolate cake that had been sitting on the counter.

"Martin, can you go in the other room and get the

cake plates out of the hutch?"

"Sure."

I got up and went into the adjacent room and started looking through the cabinet for the right plates. As I did so, I heard a buzz of whispering coming from the kitchen. I turned around to see my Mom with two hands leaning on the table standing over My Phuong. Her face looked stern, and she quickly said many things to her like a teacher scolding a student. I couldn't hear what she was saying, but I knew it wasn't good. Suddenly, My Phuong jerked her head sharply towards my Mom, stood up and let into her also in a stern, harsh tone. They stood face to face baring their teeth like two dogs on leashes wanting a chance to go at one another. My Mom said something forcefully in reply, and My Phuong emphatically jerked her head and banged the table with her fist. My Mom raised her right hand and slapped her across the face.

"Mom!" I yelled and rushed into the room.

"Get out of my house."

My Phuong turned around and ran through the living room and out of the house.

"Mom! Why? Why?"

"Martin, I won't have the likes of her in this house. Don't be so stupid. Are you blind? Can't you see what kind of person she is?"

"Mom!"

"Martin, listen to me. She's nothing but a prostitute. She's just using you. She'll never love you. You need to just wake up and stop living in a fantasy world."

My whole body ached in hatred and anger. I glared at her as tears welled up in my eyes.

"How could you?"

"Martin, you know how the Vietnam War destroyed my life. Destroyed my marriage. I cannot sit back and watch you be suckered into her deceit and lies. She doesn't love you. She'll never love you."

"Mom, I'm done. I'm done with you, and this house, and this past you've been holding onto for forty years. I will not live in it anymore. I will not be part of it, and you have shown me tonight that you want no part of my life. So stay out of it. Forever."

I turned and ran out of the house. I had to find My Phuong.

"Martin," my mom called after me.

I would not respond.

I ran down Home Avenue and turned onto Main, then down two more blocks and onto Reverend Fox's front yard when I saw My Phuong sitting at the picnic table beside the wooden steps to her apartment. I stopped and caught my breath and then approached the table and sat down beside her.

"My Phuong, I'm so sorry."

"No, Martin. It's okay."

"No, really. I'm so sorry. I will never forgive my Mother. She had no right to treat you like that."

"It's okay, really."

She looked over at me. Her face looked tired and heavy.

"My poor sweet My Phuong."

She smiled at me.

"You are the sweet one."

"What did my Mom say to you?"

"It's not important."

"What did she say?"

"Martin, I don't want to talk about it."

I stopped pressing her, but I had trouble controlling the anger inside.

"I just can't believe that she slapped you. I'm so sorry."

"Martin, really. I'm not angry. You did warn me."

"But I had no idea she would go this far. I want you to know that I'm through with my mother. I'm moving out, and I'm not going to have anything to do with her."

"No Martin. You can't do that. She's your mother. She'll always be your mother. You still must love her."

"But I can't forgive her for what she did."

"You may not forgive her, but you still must remember that she's your mother. What she did to me is not important, okay?"

She looked at me and then put both her hands on my cheeks.

"Okay?"

"Okay," I said. But there was more I needed to say. And I had to say it now. "But My Phuong, I want you to know this. You've changed my life. No, that's not true. You've given me life. I love you."

I turned away. I felt so embarrassed, and I didn't know how to act.

"You are sweet," she said and came over and kissed me. Then she smiled in a devious sort of manner. "Come with me."

She took my hand and led me up the steps and into the small living room where I often sat to play games or watch TV.

"What do you want to do?" I asked.

"Martin, come on," she said as she pointed towards

the bedroom.

I stopped and took my hands out of hers and just fidgeted nervously for a few moments as she came back close to me and put her arms around me, or at least tried to.

"Martin, it's okay. It's been a long time for me. It's okay. I want to do this."

She had no idea what long time really meant, for I hadn't been with a girl since senior high school when I was dating Sharon Camp. She was chubby like me and we got physical one night and almost nearly did it. That was my experience. I felt coldness running down my spine.

"What is it? Don't you find me attractive?" she said playfully.

"Your attractiveness makes me want to die."

"It's okay. Come die in my arms," and she lifted her head up towards mine and kissed me.

I felt sick. It was too much for me.

"Excuse me," I said and ran towards her bathroom. I shut the door behind me and threw up into her toilet. I sat there for a minute thinking about how pathetic I was. The girl of my dreams was giving herself to me, and I could only puke. Dad wouldn't have puked. He knew what to do when the girl smiled at him under the banana tree. He knew how to make his move and give the girl what she wanted. I sat there for ten minutes afraid to show my face to My Phuong. I finally emerged as an ashamed puppy with its tail between its legs. My Phuong sat on the couch with an expression of disbelief on her face.

"My Phuong. I'm so sorry."

"Martin Kinney, you are a mystery. There is no doubt about that."

"I'm so sorry. It's just. I don't know. I don't know what my problem is. I just thought of Reverend Fox down there, and how he would disapprove. I don't know. I just don't want to take advantage of you. I just don't want you to think that my attraction is only physical. I—"

She came over to me and put her finger over my lips.

"Martin, I'm yours. Whenever you are ready to have me, I'm yours. I'll wait."

Without thinking, it just came out of my mouth.

"Will you marry me?"

I felt a massive lump in my throat, and my heart pounded frantically. My Phuong took a step back blocking out the corner lamp behind her casting a shadow on her face. I couldn't really tell what expression looked back at me. I carelessly plopped down on the couch.

"I'm sorry, I—" I started, trying to correct or temper my absurd question. And then she stepped towards me and sat down beside me. She looked so small next to me. And then she broke the silence with the most terrifying of words.

"Yes, Martin. I will."

I stood up, smiled at my bride to be, and ran back into the bathroom.

Preparations

Nothing my mother said or did would ever matter again. She could no longer hurt us. I would have a new life with My Phuong.

I fell asleep on My Phuong's couch that night, and she placed a blanket over me and then went and slept in her own bed. Early in the morning she was in the kitchen making me breakfast. I paused to wonder if I really had a fiancée; I believed I did.

She came over to me with an exuberant walk, more like hopping than anything else.

"How is my future husband this morning?"

"I'm in love. And I can't believe it is true."

"Well, it is. And I think we should get married soon. What about you?"

"Yes, I don't want to delay," I said. "I don't need a big wedding."

"Simple. Let's keep it simple."

"Would it be all right with you if we got married here, in Reverend Fox's church?"

"I think my father would have liked that."

"Let's go talk to Reverend Fox."

"After breakfast," she said and kissed me on the cheek.

And so after twenty minutes, we stood at Reverend Fox's cinderblock front steps and waited for him to answer.

"Good morning Martin, My Phuong."

"Reverend, we are sorry to disturb you so early, but could we talk to you about something? It's important," I asked.

"Of course, come on in."

My Phuong and I sat back down beside each other in the love seat while the Reverend went to his regular rocker.

"Reverend, I have asked My Phuong to marry me, and she has said 'yes'."

"Well, that's wonderful. Congratulations! I'm so pleased to hear this," he said standing up and walking over to shake my hand. "And can I hug the bride to be?"

My Phuong stood up and hugged Reverend Fox. He then went back and sat down in his chair.

"Reverend Fox," My Phuong started. "As you know, my father was a pastor. And I know that he would have wanted me to be married in a church. I know that I haven't followed all the wishes my father would have had for my life, but I know that he would want this. Would you honor us by marrying us?"

"It would be my privilege and honor to conduct the wedding ceremony for you. Have you set a date?"

"This month."

"This month? Wow. Isn't that a little fast?"

"Yes, it is," I acknowledged. "But we don't want to

wait. We've been waiting our whole lives. It just feels right."

"Are you both sure?"

"Yes, Reverend," added My Phuong. "This is what we want."

We chatted for a while and decided to get married two weeks from Saturday. Reverend Fox then suggested that since the time was short, he could ask some of the deaconesses at church to plan a simple wedding reception that could take place in the church's basement fellowship hall. We readily agreed with his idea.

"Why don't you two spend some time over the next few days to determine what your ceremony should be like? Then we can meet next Tuesday and plan everything out. Okay?"

"That sounds great, Reverend. Thank you so much."

"My pleasure. Martin, what about your mother? Does she know yet?"

"No."

"How do you think she is going to take it?"

"Reverend, she will be as angry as usual. We had a dinner together last evening, and it was terrible. I'm moving out of the house. I can't stay there anymore."

"I am sorry Martin. I will pray for the situation. Now where will you live until the wedding?"

"I don't know. I haven't decided yet."

The Reverend leaned forward and had an intense look on his face making the wrinkles around his eyes very prominent.

"Martin, I hate to be so forward about things," the Reverend continued. "But I do want it to be clear that you can't stay in the apartment with My Phuong – at least not until you are married."

"No, no. Reverend. Of course not."

My Phuong let out a small laugh. I suppose she was thinking of me throwing up in the bathroom.

"It's just that we have to keep the specter of propriety. You understand how we couldn't have inappropriate things going on in the church's apartment."

Very little chance of that happening.

"Of course Reverend. But, might I ask. After we are married, would it be all right for me to move into the apartment for a while until we find someplace else?"

"Yes, you may both stay as long as you like. We'll work out a rent schedule for you."

Over the next couple of days, we planned out the details of the wedding. The guest list consisted exclusively of my side of the family which meant it would be a very small wedding. There were a couple of guys from work, a few neighbors and a few bowling buddies. We estimated about twenty people would come. I debated on whether I should inform my mother. I didn't want to. I had been avoiding her since the dinner by dropping by the house during my lunch break, getting clothes and necessities and bringing them over to my friend's house where I'd been staying. My Phuong insisted that I needed to tell her. She said that my mother had to be invited no matter what she had done.

"But how could you accept her presence after what she did to you," I asked her.

"It is nothing. Mother-in-laws are meant to be protective of their sons. It is the way of the world. I as the new daughter-in-law have to learn to endure and one day perhaps she will accept me. This is the way of Vietnam. I can bear it."

I had a lot of trouble understanding her logic, but I agreed that I would notify my Mom.

The other issue I had secretly been working on was to find an engagement ring and wedding bands. For several days after work I had been hitting the jewelry stores in Butler and up at the mall until I finally decided on a simple half-carat diamond with white gold. I had planned on just giving it to her the day of our wedding since she didn't have that custom in Vietnam and certainly wasn't expecting one. But after sleeping with it under my pillow for three nights, I couldn't bear it any longer. On day ten of our engagement, which was the midway point to our wedding, I took her back to Alameda Park where we had our first walk and talk and sat her down in one of the swings. I kneeled down in front of her, and she had this curious look on her face.

"My Phuong, I'm sorry I didn't do this properly the first time. But now I have something for you. This ring is a symbol of my love for you, and it is a promise that I will do everything to be the kind of husband that you deserve. So this is for you. Will you still marry me?"

Her face lit up with joy. She took the jewelry box in her hand and opened it, placing the delicate finger tips of her right hand on the diamond.

"Martin, a diamond. It's beautiful. Yes, yes, I will still marry you."

She jumped out of the swing and into my arms. I stood up, and held her with my arms around her. Her feet dangled off the ground. She felt as light as child. Then we kissed.

I was now down to the last task I needed to

accomplish in preparation of our wedding – informing my mother. On the Saturday prior to the ceremony, I stopped by the house around noon and Mom was in the kitchen.

"Martin?" she said as I opened the door. "Is that you?"

I didn't say anything but walked slowly into the kitchen wearing a rather grim face.

"Where have you been staying?"

"I've been staying over at Derrick's house."

"Martin, you can live here. You should live here."

"No, I think this is for the best."

"Are you still seeing that girl? I didn't ruin anything for you, did I?" she asked with a slight hint of haughtiness. It was her way of getting information.

"Mom, I have something to tell you. My Phuong and I are getting married."

My Mom looked at me but remained surprisingly emotionless and calm.

"Next Saturday at the Methodist Church. Reverend Fox is performing the ceremony."

She nodded as if she understood everything I said, but she didn't reply.

"I wanted you to know. I know that we haven't been in agreement about things, but you are still my mother, and I thought you should know."

"So I take it my wishes in this matter are meaningless?"

"I know you probably wouldn't feel comfortable coming, but if you want to, you can. I just wanted you to know."

"What time is it?"

"One o'clock."

"And you are sure this will make you happy, Martin?"

"Yes. I love her."

She didn't say anything else. I stood awkwardly in the middle of the floor for a moment.

"I have to get a few things. I'll be moving the rest of my things after the wedding. We are going to be staying in the apartment at the church at least for a while."

For once there was no yelling or inappropriate language. Even though the tension was palpable, it had gone much better than I had expected. When I pulled out of the driveway, Mom was sitting on the front porch, and I waved to her. She waved back.

As the wedding crept closer, we concentrated on getting every last preparation right. On Sunday afternoon, My Phuong met with a few of the ladies from church who had planned to hold a small reception after the ceremony. One lady had a cousin who ran a bakery and agreed to give us an excellent discount on a small wedding cake. The other ladies agreed to organize some finger foods and snacks as we decided against a formal sit-down gathering. We were very appreciative of Reverend Fox's congregation for pitching in with so many of the details. Once Reverend Fox conveyed the nature of My Phuong's background of religious persecution, many people volunteered eagerly to help although some seemed perplexed why she never attended any of the church services. She kept telling them that she would but at the last minute found some excuse to withdraw. We both continued working during the day and then spending our evenings watching TV if there were no wedding preparations to complete.

On Wednesday evening three days before the wedding, we sat in our familiar spot on the couch watching a cooking show. My Phuong had her glass of beer in her hand, and I had my arm around her.

"Martin, you never did tell me why you don't drink," she asked while taking a sip. "Don't you like beer?"

"Actually, I do like the taste of it."

"Then, why don't you drink?"

My dad. He ultimately was the reason why I did or didn't do many things in my life.

"Well, you met my Mom, and you know what she is capable of. My dad was worse. He was a severe alcoholic getting drunk every night after work. I don't even know how he kept his job all those years. When I was a teen, my dad would get beer for me and friends all the time, so we would party like foolish high school kids. After high school I would continue to drink with my friends getting drunk from time to time. It was in 1996, on a Tuesday night. I had been at the bowling alley, of course, and we had been playing and drinking. I had had way too much to drink, but I got in my car anyways and drove home. I pulled onto Home Avenue and I couldn't negotiate the turn and I went right into the Smith's mailbox and right up on their lawn. I staggered out of the car, and I just walked the rest of the way home leaving the car there. I didn't know what I was doing. I walked into the house and my Mom saw my condition immediately and started slapping me across the face like she always did with dad. I stumbled into the living room and fell onto the sofa and slept. About an hour later, I heard my name being called so I looked up still partially asleep and I saw my dad laying on the floor right at the foot of the sofa. Then I looked over to the door and there stood a police officer. I tried to stand up, but as I did I stumbled over dad and fell down to my knees. The

officer turned out to be a friend of my dad's, if you can
believe that. He took me out to the front porch and
sternly reprimanded me. I felt so ashamed. He said he
would only give me a warning if I promised to never drink
and drive again and if I fixed the Smith's mailbox and yard.
I agreed, and he left. I remember walking back into the
living room and just looking at my dad out cold. It scared
me half to death that I was going to turn into him."

My Phuong patted my arm and looked up at me in a
loving glance.

"You are nothing like your father."

"I have never taken a drink since that day."

"I'm very proud of you Martin," she said as she
opened another beer and poured it into her glass.

"Does it bother you that I drink?"

"No, just as long as you don't start abusing me," I
jabbed.

"Oh, no," she said. "The beer is making me drunk. I
think I'm going to be angry. Martin," she raised her voice.
"Martin, you've been a naughty boy. I'm going to have to
punish you."

She started hitting my arm and laughing out loud.

"I'm out of control, Martin."

"Yes, but are you ticklish?"

I poked her stomach and she let out a scream and
jolted backwards.

"You are ticklish, aren't you?"

"No, no. Leave me alone, or I'll abuse you."

"Ahh," I attacked her side with my index finger and
she screamed as she jerked upwards.

"You stop it!"

"I see your weakness."

She held her beer above her head trying not to spill it.

"Martin, you are going to make me spill."

"That's all right. This place has a good maid."

"Why you—"

As she went to even the score with a blow to my side, the cell phone in my right pocket started ringing.

"Wait, wait," I said. "Let me get this."

I reached to get my phone, but it got caught on the creases of my pocket. I pulled it out with a large tug and answered.

"Hello. Mom?" I said sitting back swiftly that my large arm crashed into My Phuong with such force that the beer spilled all over her shirt.

"Oh, I'm sorry," I said. "No, wait, not you Mom. I just … can you just wait a second?"

I put my hand over the receiver.

"I'm sorry, My Phuong."

"No matter, Mr. Clumsy. I'll change," she said, kissing me on the cheek.

"Tell your Mother I said 'hello'," she whispered in a sultry manner in my ear and stood up, walking over towards the bedroom.

"Mom, what is it?"

"Martin, I want to talk to you about this wedding."

My Phuong had turned around looking directly at me. Her shirt was stained and soaked in beer. She had a playful grin on her face.

"Mom, there is nothing to talk about."

"Martin, I'm still your mother and I need you to listen to me."

My Phuong mouthed something to me about my mother, but I couldn't understand what she meant.

"Mom, you have been incredibly unfair to me and My Phuong, so I don't think we have anything to talk about."

Then she did it. My Phuong grabbed her soaked shirt by the bottom and flipped it up over her head. My eyes bulged out, and I froze, looking upon her in only her bra. She twirled the shirt over her head a few times.

"Martin, Martin. Did you hear anything that I just said? Martin."

"Sorry, honey," My Phuong cooed at me in an innocent voice. "I didn't mean to make you sick to the stomach. The bathroom is right over there."

She laughed out loud then quickly turned and sauntered into the bedroom and closed her door.

"Martin."

I felt anything but nauseous. My blood pumped through my body like never before. For the first time I felt that I could match up to My Phuong in a physical manner. My fear subsided, though I trembled greatly.

"Mom, I gotta go."

"Martin, don't hang up on me. Mart—"

I hung up and went over to the bedroom door. I knocked and waited. She opened the door twirling her long black hair and cocking her head back and forth. She wore a new shirt.

"Yes, how may I help you?"

"Ah, I thought that maybe ... I thought."

"No, no, no. We need to take care of that sensitive stomach of yours. Plus, the show is back on. We still have to learn how to make lasagna. You'll just have to wait until after the wedding."

She walked over to the couch swinging her hips in such a cruel way as she walked. A good cruel. A wonderful cruel. I would wait for her.

"So what did your mother want? Did you thank her for the stains on my chest?"

"I don't know. You made me hang up."

"Good boy," she pinched my cheeks and kissed me lightly on the lips. "Shhh, no more non-sense. We have to watch."

I watched her the rest of the evening and could think of nothing else but her silhouette standing in her bedroom door frame. Cruel.

Mom tried calling me again on Thursday and Friday, but I just let it ring. I would make no overtures to her until after we were married. And then if she wanted to be part of our life, maybe we could try her out on a trial basis.

Late Friday afternoon I showed up at My Phuong's apartment, and to my great surprise, my friend Derrick and George were there. They were sitting on my couch drinking My Phuong's beer and laughing as I entered.

"There's the man," said George.

"One more day of freedom and then you have to hang out with this girl for the rest of your life."

"What are you guys doing here?"

"They came to give you your bachelor party," My Phuong said proudly.

"No, no. I don't need a bachelor party."

Derrick stood up and came over to me.

"The man who says he doesn't need a bachelor party is exactly the kind of man who needs one."

"That's right," said George. "There's this great joint down in the 'Burgh. The ladies will be hot all night long."

"George, not in front of," I used my head to point at My Phuong.

She laughed and came over to me.

"Martin, I want you to go and have a good time. Don't worry about me. This is your last night of freedom. After that, I'm going to be the bitchy wife," she laughed.

"No, I—"

"You can't stay here anyways. I don't want to see you anymore until I walk down the aisle tomorrow and see my handsome husband in his black suit standing in front of me. Now go."

"My Phuong, don't worry. We'll take good care of him," George said as he started pushing me out of the apartment.

"My Phuong —"

"Martin, it's okay. You go and have fun."

She came over to me and motioned for George and Derrick to leave. She then put her arms part way around me.

"Tomorrow night, we'll have our own fun, and no stomach ailment will stop us. Okay?"

"Okay," I said. "I love you."

"I know," she said.

We kissed.

"Now go."

I didn't want to leave her. I had never expected to have anything remotely close to a bachelor party, and something about it make me feel uneasy. I didn't want to go see any girls or do anything crazy. I only wanted one girl.

"Martin, we are going to take you to Sparks down route 19. And yes, the sparks are going to fly. You are going to see some women, and—"

"No. Guys, I appreciate what you are doing. Really, I

do, but I don't want to go see any women. It just wouldn't be right. I want to be faithful to My Phuong."

They both looked at each other in disbelief.

"But," Derrick tried to say something.

"I'm serious. I won't go to anyplace like that. Can we just do something else?"

"Like what?" asked George who seemed rather disappointed.

I thought for a moment.

"Actually, I would like nothing better than to go bowling with you guys. One last bowling night as a single man."

"You want tacos, don't you?"

"You know it. I want a dozen tacos, and a six-pack of Cherry Coke."

Derrick smiled.

"You are just too predictable. But it sounds like fun. Let's go."

We got into George's Camaro and rode down to the lanes for one last crazy night of singlehood.

The Day

Saturday morning – my wedding day. The previous evening we had bowled and ate for about three hours and then came back to Derrick's house to watch movies until early into the morning. I talked to My Phuong once in the evening on the phone and I told her that we didn't go and look at girls. She thought I was sweet. Around nine, I woke up, ate breakfast and put on my black suit – the only one I had – the one I wore to dad's funeral three years ago. It actually hung a little loose on me. I nervously walked around in the suit all morning counting down each and every minute. Earlier in the week, Derrick's mother asked me if I wanted help choosing a boutonnière. After she explained what one was, I thanked her for her help and simply requested that it was red just like the Phuong flower. At eleven o'clock, she helped me attach the red boutonniere onto my lapel. At eleven-thirty, I got in the car with Derrick and drove over to the church. We met Reverend Fox in his office to wait out the final hour. I asked him about My Phuong, and he told me that Mrs. Presley was helping her get ready in the back room. I was grateful that she had someone to help her. I felt sorry that her family couldn't have been here, and then I reminded myself that I too had no family coming. But it didn't matter. Once we were married, we would have each other and that was enough.

At 12:30, Reverend Fox came back in the room carrying a large envelope.

"Martin, here is the marriage license. Can you sign it?"

He placed it on the edge of his desk and handed me a pen.

"Right here," he pointed down to a dotted line.

Right underneath the line was My Phuong's signature. I marveled at how the stroke of a pen changes everything. I signed my name Martin J. Kinney Jr. We were married. I was a thirty-nine year old married man – married to a beautiful Vietnamese woman, whom I loved more than life itself. I thought for a moment about what had brought me to this day. Dad's story about Newbert and Johnson – the girl under the banana tree – the promise to dad – the misunderstanding of the words Tay Nguyen – the wallet. It all purposed me to this point where I would never be the same. I stood on the brink of tears just looking at the signed marriage license.

"Martin, everything okay?" asked the Reverend.

"Yes, it's perfect."

"It's time."

I nodded. Derrick and I followed the Reverend out of his study to the front of the center aisle. I counted twenty one people in attendance, but my Mother was not among them. Mrs. Grassley started the wedding march on the organ and everyone stood to attention and focused on the back of the church. I finally saw her. She stood in the archway wearing a long, flowing white *ao dai*. There was no veil. Her hair was fixed up in a bun. She stood so dainty, so frail-like, as beautiful as an angel. She moved towards me slowly and her white *ao dai* flowed smoothly. I remembered how she disappeared as a vapor amongst the festival crowd in Thai Nguyen trying to escape me. But now she moved purposefully, with her eyes fixed upon me, trying to get to me. The walk seemed to take so long. I just wanted her beside me. I wanted the Reverend to pronounce us husband and wife. I wanted to kiss her. I wanted her to be mine, forever and ever.

She reached the front and stood on my left. As Reverend Fox said a prayer of blessing, we just looked at each other. She smiled funny at me and softly touched her cheek to let me know that she recognized that I had shaved. It was the first time it was smooth in many years. Then she lipped something to me. Something she had never said before. I'm sure I read her lips correctly. She formed the words 'I love you'. The Reverend finished his prayer and we turned towards him.

"We are gathered today to witness the marriage of Martin J. Kinney Jr. and My Phuong Nong in holy matrimony. A strange twist of events have occurred in their lives to bring them to the point of wanting to join together in marriage to become one as the Bible teaches. Perhaps fitting, this marriage more than anything is a symbol of a journey because two very different journeys have created the foundation on which this marriage is about to be made. Three years ago, many of us stood at this same spot and honored the passing of Martin's father. He left Martin with one request, bury his ashes in Vietnam. Martin obeyed the will of his father, perhaps even against advice and his own better judgment, and stepped far out of his comfort zone to see that wish fulfilled. In doing so, he had a brief, chance encounter with the Vietnamese woman – My Phuong – standing before us today. My Phuong, as it turned out, had been on a journey of her own. Her family was persecuted for their faith for doing simple things like worshipping publicly – actions that we take far too much for granted here in America. She had to run away for safety. She survived an arduous trip to America and unfair treatment once she arrived. But from the day she showed up at Martin's door, these two have exhibited love at its best. Love that doesn't prejudge, love that understands, love that cares, love that is self-sacrificing, love that is relational. I am so pleased to stand here today and bring together two very special individuals who deserve each other and who deserve happiness."

He looked and nodded over to Lola Meyers who stood beside Mrs. Grassely sitting at the piano. The piano started and then Lola began singing the Bee Gees' *How Deep is Your Love* – a special request of My Phuong from all her days singing Karaoke. I barely heard any of the song. I could only concentrate on that angelic face in front of me.

At the end of the song, Reverend Fox opened his Bible and turned to I Corinthians 13 and read the love chapter also specially requested from My Phuong.

"Love is patient, love is kind, it does not envy, it does not boast ..."

I thought for sure everyone would envy me, and I wanted to boast to the world about my bride. She was so patient to tolerate me, and she was ever so kind.

After the Reverend finished reading the chapter, he

asked us to turn and face each other and clasp hands together. We then repeated our vows, one at a time, gazing right into each other's eyes.

"Martin, do you have a symbol of your love?"

"Yes, this ring."

Derrick handed me the gold band, and I placed it on her left ring finger.

"And My Phuong, do you have a symbol of your love?"

"Yes, this ring."

Lola walked over to My Phuong and handed her the ring and then placed it on my left ring finger.

"This ring is a symbol of eternal love with no ending and no beginning," Reverend Fox continued.

Out of the corner of my eye, I saw a few people in the congregation turning around and whispering about something. Then Reverend Fox stopped speaking and looked directly past us down the aisle. I turned my head to the left and saw her approaching – my mother. My Phuong dropped my hand which she held and turned around towards her as well. A slight buzz of commotion rippled through the small crowd and all eyes were fixed on my mother. She was dressed in a Sunday outfit and held her pocketbook under her right arm. She walked slowly towards us in a steady pace with her eyes fixed on me.

"Mom," I said walking two steps towards her then stopping. "You came. You can sit up here in the front."

I motioned my hand towards the front left pew, but she had taken her eyes off of me and stopped about fifteen feet in front of My Phuong. I cringed to think that she was going to make a scene. I heard nothing from the Reverend, who now stood to my back.

"I will not let you ruin my family," she said looking

straight at My Phuong.

"Mom, stop this. Now," I said as my heart filled with despair and anger. I could not believe that this was happening again. I refused to believe that she could ruin the greatest day of my life.

"Vietnam ruined my family once. I will not allow it to happen again."

"Mom!"

As I yelled out at her, she reached into her pocketbook and pulled out a handgun and quickly pointed it. CRACK. The shot reverberated from every direction off the ceiling and walls. People screamed and dove down behind the pews. The bullet hit My Phuong with such force that she went flying backwards and landed against the altar. Her body lay twisted with her arms and legs going in different directions. The sound closed in on me until my mind drowned everything out. My ears felt like a great fullness had entered them. I felt dizzy and lost my balance falling down to one knee. My mother kept holding the gun pointing it towards the front of the church.

"And you," she said now aiming at Reverend Fox. "It's all your doing, too."

Her hand shook up and down. The Reverend stood crying, shaking his head back and forth, pleading for mercy.

Suddenly, my mom dropped the gun to the floor and stood coldly with her arms down at her sides, not moving. One of the church elders who cowered behind a pew just a few feet away from her lunged for the gun and secured it. Two other individuals came and grabbed my mother's arms and pulled them tightly behind her back holding her captive.

I looked over at My Phuong. Blood, bright red blood, flowed down the front of her beautiful white *ao dai*. I rose to my feet and ran to her, picked her up and put her into my arms rocking her, talking to her, crying at her. Reverend Fox came to my side and quickly put his suit jacket on top of My Phuong as if to stop the bleeding. Movement and sound surrounded me, cornering me on all sides, but I could only see and comprehend two things – my lovely My Phuong with a red stained chest, bleeding to death in my arms, and my mom staring at me expressionless from the center aisle.

I don't remember what happened in the next few minutes. It wasn't long though until I saw uniformed policemen and paramedics coming towards me. They took My Phuong out of my arms placing her on a gurney. They worked on her chest and shouted back and forth. They tried to revive her and keep her stable, but she lay lifeless in front of me. I sat against the altar and wept. Reverend Fox wept right beside me with his arm around my neck. There was nothing anybody could do. My Phuong was dead.

Home

Nothing heals the wounds from a tragedy such as this. There are no prayers of comfort, no silver linings, no moral lessons to be learned. At night I went to sleep. In the morning I woke up. It was only in these mundane tasks that my life had any meaning. There was nothing more. Nothing at all.

Reverend Fox took me into his house those first few days after the incident. He didn't want me to be alone. Every morning I would walk out of the house, and the church building would stab me with reality. I felt sick every hour of every day. Every evening I sat on the picnic table out near the steps to her apartment which was the closest thing to sacred ground my family would ever know. So much pain and promise went up and down that staircase, but it was once again vacant. I wouldn't go up to the apartment. I didn't want to see her belongings, and I didn't want to sit in the places which once were the most magical places in the world for me.

I couldn't stay focused on anything. I sat, and I walked. I drove around town and did everything in my power to ignore the lawyers who tried to contact me. I wanted nothing to do with them or anyone else. Reverend Fox became my only conduit to the outside world. He made all the necessary arrangements concerning My Phuong's death. When he asked me what my wishes were, I told him that I wished this whole thing didn't happen, and I asked the typical questions about God's presence that the victims of tragedies so often voice.

On the third day of my new life, I sat at the familiar picnic table and Reverend Fox came up from behind me without me noticing him. He placed My Phuong's urn right in front of me without saying a word. My eyes fixated on it, but there were no tears left within me. I stared at it feeling nothing but emptiness.

"Martin," Reverend Fox jolted my consciousness. "Martin. What are you going to do?"

I sat, unresponsive having no idea of what to say. He sat down across from me.

"I can't tell you what to do, Martin. But in your own time and in your own way, you need to bring closure to this part of your life. You can stay here as long as you like." He stopped and looked at me. I kept my eyes on the urn. "If you want to have some sort of memorial service—"

"No," I said abruptly. I didn't want to look into my neighbors' eyes and fake a smile of appreciation for them coming to pay their respects. I didn't want to hear Reverend Fox's words ring hollow. If my dad were here, he would know how to use some vulgar phrase to sum up my feelings really well. That is what I needed, not some memorial service.

"Okay, Martin. Just so you know. You can stay as long

as you like. My home is your home."

The Reverend stood up and walked silently back to his house.

Home. That last word reverberated inside me, and it wasn't long until it finally hit me hard and clear. The obvious had been staring me in the face for days now, but I was too caught up in my emotions to see it. I knew now more than ever what I had to do, and there was no time to waste.

I got into my car and drove over to Home Avenue and parked in front of my house. Urn in hand, I went in the front door, through the living room, and into the kitchen. I pulled a large red-lid Rubbermaid container from the cabinet and placed it on the table. I opened My Phuong's urn and very carefully poured the ashes into the container spilling nothing in the process. Then I grabbed a Ziploc from the bottom drawer and ran upstairs to my bedroom. In my closet, under my hanging clothes and on the bottom shelf sat dad's urn. I pulled it out and sat on the floor, opened the Ziploc wide and balancing it delicately on the floor, I poured out the remaining ashes of dad which hadn't fit the first time around. I zipped it up, ran downstairs and placed the bag on top of My Phuong's ashes already in the container. Then I closed the lid and sealed it all with blue duct tape.

I made two phone calls. The first was to K-Mart to tell them that I quit. The second was to AAA to book my flight. I then grabbed Mom's debit card from her purse in the desk, drove down to the bank and withdrew the maximum amount allowed, which was a considerable sum. Within three days, I was packed and ready to go.

On Sunday morning, the eighth day after the incident,

I arrived at Tan Son Nhat Airport in Ho Chi Minh City – the former capital of South Vietnam. It had been nearly forty-four years since another Kinney had been in this location. It was still very early in the morning. I went promptly to the taxi counter and hired a car to take me to Tay Nguyen – Dak Lak Province – Ban Me Thuot town. I threw my backpack into the trunk and put my shoulder bag containing the Rubbermaid container on the seat next to me behind the driver. We drove for hours and hours through the countryside. Peasants and water buffaloes dotted the landscape readying the fields for another planting. We travelled up the coast past Nha Trang until we finally turned west up into the highlands.

"How far are we from Ban Me Thuot?" I eventually asked the taxi driver who hadn't spoken a word to me since the airport.

"About seventy kilometers."

"These house on stilts, are these a different ethnic group?"

"Huh?"

"Who lives here? Vietnamese?"

The driver still didn't understand me.

"*Kinh*?" I pointed out to the fields with rice paddies and with long houses on stilts towered out of the trees perched on the rolling hills in the background. I had learned the word *kinh* from My Phuong. It meant the ethnic Vietnamese – the majority of people in Vietnam.

"No, no, not *kinh*. These are the Mnong."

"The Mnong?"

"Yes."

I still wasn't sure, so I pulled a receipt out of my wallet and scribbled M-N-O-N-G on it and showed it to him.

"Yes, Mnong."

"Can you pull over? I want to see some of them."

"No, no. Buon Me Thuot one hour. We stop there."

"No, I want to stop here."

"No, nothing here."

"Stop the car."

"Nothing here."

"Pull over here," I said forcefully.

Finally, the driver said a few words under his breath and pulled off to the side. I really missed Tan. Between two rice paddies was a small elevated dirt road which wound out of sight through the woods on the hill. Several houses on stilts were visible on the right.

"Drive down there."

"No, my car can't go down there."

"Go!"

He complained some more under his breath, and we went bumping up and down, in and out of the potholes.

"Not good for the car," he said and continued to complain the whole way. I ignored him and just watched two small boys who sat on top of a grey buffalo in the rice field. They waved furiously at me, and I waved back.

We finally pulled up around a cluster of five or six houses. Several people were standing around and several more came down the steps of the houses to look at the tall, fat, red-headed American step out of the taxi. I smiled at the people and nodded my head. They chattered fiercely and stared at me. I looked around and noticed that one of the houses had a cross hanging over the windows.

"Hello. Does anyone speak English?"

Several little boys walked up to me and mimicked

"hello, hello" but seemed to know no other words. I turned to the driver who was standing beside the car smoking.

"Can you ask them in Vietnamese if anyone speaks English?"

"*Co ai noi Tieng Anh o day khong*?"

A couple of men chatted in the background and yelled into one of the houses. A moment later, a young man, perhaps in his late twenties and wearing glasses, came down the house steps, exchanged words with the old men and then approached me.

"Hello. I speak English. Can I help you?"

"Yes. Is this a Christian village?"

"Yes, it is. We have small church over the hill there."

"I'm looking for the church of a man who was arrested by the police about four years ago."

"Pardon?" the young man asked for clarification.

"Let me write it for you."

I handed him a slip of paper that read 'Mnong pastor – four years ago – arrested by police – do you know him?' He looked at it at length and then went over to two elderly men and translated what was written on the paper to them. The elderly men were very animated and kept pointing over the hill.

"Yes. We know. His name is Nong Klung. His church is only five kilometers from here. I can take you there."

"His church? He has a church?"

"Yes, today Wednesday. He at home for sure. I take you there."

"No, sorry. That is the wrong person."

I thought for a moment I might have gotten lucky when he said they knew him, but when I heard he was alive, I knew it was a mistake.

"You don't want to go?"

"Well, do you know if Nong Klung had any children?"

The young man turned back to the elderly men and chatted for a minute.

"He has two sons and one daughter."

It was a good try I thought to myself.

"But his daughter disappeared about four years ago. Nobody knows where she is."

My heart pounded. Could it really be true? I had to find out for sure.

"Take me to him."

"Okay, but we can't go by taxi. We go back way on foot."

"Okay."

I went back to the taxi and took out my large backpack and my one shoulder bag. I decided to jump in feet first with no turning back because I had nothing to lose. I told the driver I was finished with him, and I started walking with the young man into the forest. A trail of children clipped my heels at every turn. One of them caught up with me and handed me a bunch of bananas. Others would try to sneak up behind me to rub the hair on my arms. They were the cutest little kids, and I didn't care what they did to me. I even found myself smiling at them from time to time.

We walked on a small trail up through the lush vegetation. After about thirty minutes of heart-pounding walking, we climbed a steep embankment on the muddy trail, and the young man paused at the clearing on top. I huffed and puffed my way there and then bent over with my hands on my knees trying to catch my breath.

"What's your name?" I asked him.

"My name is Long."

"How did you learn English?"

"My father work very hard so I can go to better school near Ban Me Thuot. I get to study English there, plus I take more English classes at night."

"How much farther to the church?"

"It's just down there. In bottom of valley."

"Do you know the pastor?"

"Sure, I know Pastor Nong."

"What about his family? Did you know his daughter?"

"No, he's only been here a short time. I met his sons but never his daughter.

I still couldn't believe what I sincerely hoped in my heart.

We trekked down the slippery slope and after another forty minutes we came to a cluster of houses with a rather large church standing in the center. *This can't be it,* I said to myself. *My Phuong's father didn't pastor in a church building.*

Several people came and greeted us as we entered the village. Long talked with them and then led me over to the church building. We walked up the four wooden steps and entered a long structure which had wooden walls, open windows, and bamboo floors in which you could look right through the cracks and see the ground below it. I wondered if I would soon be looking up at them since the thin strips of bamboo seemed to give way so much, but they continued to hold me as we walked to the front.

A short older gentleman with a round face, bald head and a kind smile approached us. Long exchanged greetings with him and he came over to me and held out both hands to shake.

"Wel-come," he greeted in broken English.

"Hello."

Student Long explained a few more things about me and then they whisked me to the back of the church where they rolled out a mat and invited me to sit. Before I knew it, a tea cup filled with piping hot strong green tea was in my hand.

"This is Pastor Nong."

"My name is Martin."

We both nodded our heads and smiled.

"Can you ask him if he knows a girl named My Phuong?"

As he translated, I pulled out a photograph of her and held it up to him. He immediately took it out of my hands, and his countenance changed as tears of joy started streaming down his face. He exchanged some words with Long then Long confirmed it all.

"That is his daughter. Where is she? How do you know her?"

My poor My Phuong. I felt sick for her. I had found my way back to her home – the one she never knew she had. I sat across from her father, tears streaming down my face, and glanced deeply into my soul to see if I had the strength to tell him the truth.

"I'm sorry," I trembled, my voice shaken, weak and raspy. "She is dead."

Long's face became stern and mournful. He glanced at Pastor Nong and dreaded being the messenger. His head fell toward the floor, and without looking at all at the expectant pastor, he mumbled some soft subtle words – easily spoken to help dampen the blow. But soft words can usher a blow of brute force. Pastor Nong, raised his hands to the sky, then fell to the ground, face tucked in the bamboo floor, and wept. I sat stunned, and my stomach felt upset. I breathed heavily looking at the love of a father being poured out from the very depths of his being. After a minute, Pastor Nong lifted his head and whispered something to Long.

"He wants to know what happened to her."

What could I say? I looked at Long.

"She told me about the day that Pastor Nong was arrested. And she told me how she went to the authorities and asked about you, but they informed her that her parents were dead. After that, she ran away and never came back."

Long relayed everything, and Pastor Nong got very animated.

"Pastor Nong said that his wife did die in prison, but that he was released about one year ago and then came to pastor this small church in the village. He wants to know everything that happened to her."

We spent the next two hours translating the story of My Phuong's last four years. I was careful not to say anything about the ordeals that My Phuong endured in Thai Nguyen. I told them that she went to school and won a scholarship to come to America. They seemed to believe it. But when it came to her death, I couldn't tell them the truth. I couldn't bear to tell them the absolute truth. So I told them that we had married which was true. I had the marriage certificate and a wedding band to prove it. But shortly after that she was involved in a terrible traffic accident and lost her life.

Pastor Nong had been holding both of my hands

ring the whole story.

"I have something for you," I said directly to Pastor Nong.

I removed my hands from Pastor Nong's gentle clasp, and I reached into my shoulder bag and pulled out the large Rubbermaid container with duct tape all around it. I pulled off the tape and then opened it up. In one of life's more uncouth moments, I turned around to try and shield what I was doing and then pulled dad's Ziploc off the top and placed it in a handkerchief and slipped it quickly back into my bag. I just kind of smiled at them without any explanation. I put the lid back on and turned around and handed it to Pastor Nong.

"These are My Phuong's ashes. I thought you would want them."

Pastor Nong held the container in his hand and just looked at it for a few moments. Finally, he placed them on the floor and came over and hugged me many, many times. Long kept saying "thank you, thank you" over and over again.

"He says you will stay. You must stay for as long as you like. You are part of our family. Will you stay?"

"Okay," I said. "I can stay for a night."

"Yes, you will stay."

That evening, the whole village showed up at the church for prayer meeting. They all had heard the fantastic story about the strange American who had married Pastor Nong's long lost daughter. They also wanted to bury My Phuong. They sang many hymns and Long did his best to translate what he could. After the singing, Pastor Nong stood up and gave an impassioned talk about God's plans. He told all about how My Phuong had finally come home and that now she is in a better place. I hoped he was right. She deserved to be someplace better, but the whole service left me feeling sad. I just missed her.

After the service, we walked up through the hills for about ten minutes and came upon a small graveyard marked with stone crosses. They dug a hole and then Pastor Nong gave another thirty minute talk about the afterlife. When he finished, he asked me to come forward which I did with much uneasiness.

"He said that he wants his son to put the ashes in the hole."

I looked at him blankly.

"You. He considers you his son."

With a heavy heart and tears in my eyes, I took the Rubbermaid container from Pastor Nong praying beyond all hope that I wouldn't do anything clumsy with it. I opened it up, leaned over and perfectly dumped the ashes in the hole.

"Goodbye my sweet My Phuong," I whispered.

After they finished the burial and placed another cross in the ground, we walked back to the village where they gave me a feast and treated me like royalty. I felt very undeserving. Pastor Nong seemed so happy to have closure in his life, and I only wondered what closure might feel like. Around eleven at night after we had exhausted all food and talk, I lay down on a mat on the bamboo floor of Pastor Nong's house and finally nodded off.

Right around daybreak, I decided it was time to add a second layer of closure to my life. I took the handkerchief which held dad's last remains and went off over the hill looking for an appropriate spot. I walked and walked thinking about the first time I had tried to find a final resting place for dad. After about thirty minutes of wandering back and forth, I came upon a large rock jutting out of the ground. Just below the rock was a banana tree grove which immediately set my heart soaring. I ran down through the grove and within seconds I saw a large lake just one hundred or so meters away.

"Dad, I made it."

I ran back up through the grove and stood below the large rock and I imagined the beautiful girl, sitting on the rock smiling at my dad, but the only girl I could see on that rock was My Phuong. I saw her long black hair, her piercing black eyes and her clear, clean complexion. I saw the white edges of her *ao dai* shift in the wind. She waved at me and smiled, and I walked towards her just staring into her eyes. I stood at the base of the rock where my dad had his girl, and I now had mine. I opened up the Ziploc and dumped the ashes. A gust of wind whipped through the trees and the ashes spread evenly along the ground like dustings of snow.

"I did it Dad, I did it," I said as I sat down with my back against that rock. "I love you both."

I leaned my head back and cried. It was, I guess, a cry of relief more than anything. A cry of cleansing. I had nothing more to contemplate, nothing more to wrestle with, nothing more to do. The past evaporated before my eyes, and I sat as an empty vessel waiting for the sea to take me where it would. Before I knew it, I had nodded off in exhaustion.

About two hours later, a small boy and girl stood over me excitedly poking my arms trying to wake me. They talked furiously and pointed back up over the hill. They tugged on my arm, and I willingly followed. Within minutes we were back in the village, and it seemed like everyone in the whole valley stood gossiping away about the AWOL red-headed giant. They smiled and cheered when I came down the hill, and some of them even started clapping. I couldn't for the life of me figure out what all the fuss was about. Long greeted me as I entered into the circle surrounded by my adoring fans.

"So happy to see you, Mr. Martin."

"What is going on here? I don't understand."

"Everyone is so happy to see you. Pastor Nong sent word to neighboring villages telling them about the miracle of Martin. The new son of Pastor Nong who brought word about his precious daughter. Everyone wanted to come and see you for themselves."

I stood overwhelmed and embarrassed. If my face could have gotten redder, it would have. A sweet old woman came up and placed a bouquet of Phuong flowers into my hand.

"This is for you she said," Long translated. "This is My Phuong's grandmother. She says now you her grandson."

Another group of people approached me.

"This is My Phuong's uncle and aunt. They wanted to thank you."

And another group approached.

I had done nothing to deserve their praise and adoration. I had only followed my heart. Actually, I followed my selfish desires, and I followed my love for My Phuong. Perhaps I had done this all for me. I didn't deserve this treatment, but I wanted it with all my heart.

"When you were missing this morning, everyone thinks you left and aren't coming back. Everyone very afraid and sad. But now it is like a homecoming," Long said with a huge smile on his face.

Pastor Nong needled his way through the crowd towards me and tried to get everyone to settle down so he could say something.

"Martin," Long translated for me. "You are always welcome here in our village. This is your home, and we are your family. Even if you have to leave us, I know you will come back. Our village is poor, and our schools are not so good. Our children cannot compete for better jobs and better lives like those who live in the cities. We need teachers here. Our children need to learn English. Martin, would you stay with us, live with us, and teach our children English?"

Me a teacher? I barely graduated from high school.

"But tell them that I'm not a teacher. I don't know how to teach."

I laughed at their suggestion as Long translated back to them. I didn't know the first thing about teaching English.

"They said it is no problem. You are native speaker. If native speaker speak, children learn."

"But how can I stay? I only have a tourist visa, and I ..."

The absurdity of their offer kept running through my head.

"Pastor Nong says that God provided a way. Since he released from prison, and since his wife die in prison, he has good contact, good contact that help. No worry. You want to stay, you stay."

I stood there looking at their eager faces not knowing if I truly believed what the next chapter of my life would be.

"But Pastor Nong says if you have to go, it's okay. But you are always welcome here."

And then I realized what I wanted to do.

"But I have no place to go. I have no one to be with, except you."

Long translated it back to the jubilant faces.

"So you will stay?"

"I would be honored to stay."

He translated my decision, and then I heard from varying voices both young and old a single phrase repeated over and over again.

"What are they saying?" I asked.

"May God bless you! May God bless you! May God bless you!"

Over and over the phrase reverberated across the village.

A small girl jumped up into my arms and put her head on my shoulder. My Phuong's grandmother took me by the hand and started walking me to Pastor Nong's longhouse. The crowd pressed in on me from every side, but I paid no attention to my wallet, which was still sitting in the back right pocket of my jeans. I had found my way home.

CPSIA information can be obtained at www.ICGtesting.com
Printed in the USA
LVOW11s1541050114

368171LV00001B/25/P